Rafe Was A Survivor.

He would survive this trip, as he had survived gunshot wounds and raging fevers.

However, the pain would be intense.

He reviewed everything he'd learned since he'd arrived in Texas. Some of that knowledge would have been better left untouched. He'd been content with his life. Content with his solitude. Content not needing anybody, not wanting anybody.

All of that had changed now.

Now he knew what it was to wake up with Mandy in his arms. He knew the scent of her, the taste of her....

Being with her last night had been the culmination of every fantasy he'd ever dreamed since he left Texas. After this trip, he would no longer need imagination to conjure up the experience. Memories would haunt him. Forever....

Dear Reader,

Welcome to Silhouette Desire—where you're guaranteed powerful, passionate and provocative love stories that feature rugged heroes and spirited heroines who experience the full emotional intensity of falling in love!

Wonderful and ever-popular Annette Broadrick brings us September's MAN OF THE MONTH with *Lean, Mean & Lonesome*. Watch as a tough loner returns home to face the woman he walked away from but never forgot.

Our exciting continuity series TEXAS CATTLEMAN'S CLUB continues with *Cinderella's Tycoon* by Caroline Cross. Charismatic CEO Sterling Churchill marries a shy librarian pregnant with his sperm-bank baby—and finds love.

Proposition: Marriage is what rising star Eileen Wilks offers when the girl-next-door comes alive in the arms of an alpha hero. Beloved romance author Fayrene Preston makes her Desire debut with *The Barons of Texas: Tess*, featuring a beautiful heiress who falls in love with a sexy stranger. The popular theme BACHELORS & BABIES returns to Desire with Metsy Hingle's *Dad in Demand*. And Barbara McCauley's miniseries SECRETS! continues with the dramatic story of a mysterious millionaire in *Killian's Passion*.

So make a commitment to sensual love—treat yourself to all six September love stories from Silhouette Desire!

Enjoy!

Joan Marlow Golan
Senior Editor, Silhouette Desire

Please address questions and book requests to:
Silhouette Reader Service
U.S.: 3010 Walden Ave., P.O. Box 1325, Buffalo, NY 14269
Canadian: P.O. Box 609, Fort Erie, Ont. L2A 5X3

ANNETTE BROADRICK

LEAN, MEAN
& LONESOME

SILHOUETTE *Desire*®

Published by Silhouette Books

America's Publisher of Contemporary Romance

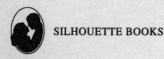 SILHOUETTE BOOKS

ISBN 0-373-76237-2

LEAN, MEAN & LONESOME

Visit us at www.romance.net

Printed in U.S.A.

Books by Annette Broadrick

ANNETTE BROADRICK

believes in romance and the magic of life. Since 1984, Annette has shared her view of life and love with readers. In addition to being nominated by *Romantic Times Magazine* as one of the Best New Authors of that year, she has also won the *Romantic Times* Reviewers' Choice Award for Best in its Series the *Romantic Times* W.I.S.H. award and the *Romantic Times* Lifetime Achievement Awards for Series Romance and Series Romantic Fantasy.

This book is dedicated to

Candy Kacena
1954-1998

I will always treasure your
beautiful gift of friendship.
You will not be forgotten.

One

A friend in need is a real pain in the ass.

Rafe McClain had muttered the thought to himself more than once in the past few days, but the utterance did nothing to change the present situation. Until the letter had arrived, Rafe hadn't given friendships much thought. He'd been a loner for a long time, which was just the way he liked it.

Then Dan Crenshaw's letter had turned up in mail that had finally found its way to him. As soon as he read the letter Rafe had been forcibly reminded of another life and time, one he'd dismissed from his conscious mind years ago.

The letter had been a plea for help and Rafe had known that, inconvenient as it was—and it was damned inconvenient—he couldn't ignore Dan's request. Thus, Rafe now battled jet lag on this, the final leg of a journey that had started many hours and time zones ago.

He scratched his cheek and made a face at the feel of the rough surface against the pads of his fingers. He should have shaved during that last layover in Atlanta on his way to Texas. It was too late, now. They'd be landing in Austin in less than an hour.

He'd been flying for two days—waiting around in airports for the next available flight. Killing time. Wishing he knew what the hell was going on to cause the summons he'd received. He was long past being tired. Hell, he didn't even know what day it was in the Central Time zone.

None of that mattered. He was doing what he could to respond to a friend's summons.

Texas.

He hated the place. He hadn't been in the state of his birth in twelve years. Not a hint of nostalgia stirred within him at the thought of his return. When he'd left with his high school diploma stuck in his back pocket, he'd vowed never to return.

So much for pledges. Dan Crenshaw was his best friend—probably his only friend if he were to be honest. They'd met in the fourth grade. The unspoken message in Dan's note was that he knew he could count on Rafe, just as Rafe had always known that Dan would be there for him if he ever needed him.

He wished Dan had been a little more specific. Other than mentioning that he could use his help and hoping to see him at the ranch soon, Dan hadn't indicated what kind of assistance he wanted or needed.

Rafe felt badly that his mail hadn't caught up with him right away. The postmark showed the letter had been mailed five weeks ago. For all Rafe knew, he could be too late with whatever help he was supposed to be offering.

He'd tried to call Dan as soon as he got the letter, but there had been no answer, no answering machine and no way of knowing whether Dan was working somewhere on the ranch or actually gone.

Rafe had seen no other choice but to head back to the

states. He had no idea whether or not his showing up at the C Bar C Ranch would accomplish anything positive.

He could think of a hell of a lot of negatives that could occur.

For one thing, he'd been warned by old man Crenshaw never to step foot on his ranch again. Of course, Dan's father had been dead for the past five years, so he supposed he could ignore that particular threat.

So, here he was, landing in Austin at ten o'clock on a hot and muggy July night, rushing to the rescue like some damned knight.

If he weren't so blasted exhausted, he'd laugh at the picture that came to mind. His armor was rusty and dented, his steed gone long ago and his lance had been smashed to smithereens. But he was there.

Once on the ground, Rafe grabbed his bag and picked up the rental car he'd reserved. Within the hour he was headed west out of town, following road signs on thoroughfares that hadn't existed when he'd lived in the area.

The ranch was located about thirty miles southwest of the state's capital in the rough and rugged hill country of Central Texas. As he drove, he was amazed to see how much expansion had taken place as civilization moved westward to claim ranch country. He noticed a Polo Club on the way, for God's sake. Polo? In Texas?

He shook his head in amusement. The times, they were definitely a-changing.

When he finally pulled up at the entrance to the ranch a while later, Rafe was more than ready to find a bed and crash for a few hours. Whatever the reason for his summons, he had a hunch it could be postponed for at least long enough for him to get some rest.

He got out of the car to open the gate and found it was padlocked. There was a large sign on the gate:

Private Property
No Trespassing

The sign and padlock were new. In the past, the combination lock had been easily opened if you knew the birthdays of Dan and Mandy, his sister.

Amanda Crenshaw. Rafe hadn't thought about her in years. She'd been fifteen the last time he'd seen her—a gangly, coltish girl with russet colored curls and an infectious smile. He had a hunch she would have as little use for him as her father had...with more reason.

Dan mentioned once that Mandy lived in Dallas, which was just as well. It would be much better for all concerned if they didn't run into each other while he was in Texas.

He studied the sign and the lock, then glanced at his watch. It was close to midnight. He could either sleep in the car and go on foot to the house in the morning, or he could make that multi-mile hike now.

Neither option particularly appealed to him.

Oh, what the hell. He returned to the car and grabbed his bag—thank God he traveled light—locked the car and climbed the fence.

He knew he was taking a chance going on the property at this time of night. In this part of the world trespassers could get shot before they had a chance to explain their presence on the premises.

If Dan wanted to shoot him he'd have to spot him first.

Rafe smiled to himself at the thought of putting into practice the training he was paid to teach in Eastern Europe. He'd see just how good he really was.

By the time he reached the ranch buildings, Rafe had slipped by two armed guards. What in the hell was going on? Rafe was beginning to get a bad feeling about all of this...a really bad feeling.

Yard lights surrounded the house. There was no way to approach it without being seen.

The house was a single story, Texas-traditional style home. Made of limestone, it had a tin roof that seemed to stretch over several acres. A long, covered porch graced the back of the place. Rafe knew the interior well, unless the family had done major renovations. Mexican tile covered the floor in most of the rooms except for the bedroom wing. A luxurious, deep-piled carpet covered the bedrooms, baths and hallway.

He recalled his youthful dreams of one day having a similar home and a loving family. Rafe was amused by those boyhood dreams, now, but they had served him well at the time, getting him through the bad patches when he was growing up.

Well, standing there admiring the place wasn't getting him any closer.

The area around the house looked free of guards but he wasn't taking any chances. He stashed his bag in some brush and began the intricate and laborious approach that would keep him from getting spotted and shot. By the time he reached the comparative shadowy area on the back porch he was royally pissed off. Mostly at himself. Why hadn't he just called and had Dan pick him up at the airport? That would have circumvented the necessity for all this sneaking around.

Suddenly all hell seemed to break loose inside the house. A large-sounding dog began a barking spree that was guaranteed to wake the dead. Rafe leaned against the wall next to the kitchen door and waited for Dan to check on why his watchdog had suddenly gone ballistic.

Amanda Crenshaw bolted out of bed as soon as Ranger started barking. Someone was out there. He didn't bark at animals. He was a trained watchdog who was now making it clear there was an intruder on the premises.

She peered out the window of her bedroom. The canine alarm should have some of the men coming to check on her soon. In the meantime, she slipped on her robe and shoes and silently made her way down the long hallway to the main part of the house.

Ranger was at the kitchen door, barking loudly. She heard a low, male voice talking in a soothing tone to him. She froze, her mind unable to accept what her heart had immediately recognized. She knew that voice. It was a voice she hadn't heard in years, one she'd never expected to hear again.

With something like panic, Mandy peered through the glass of the back door as she turned on the kitchen light.

A tall, lean man stepped away from the side of the house when he saw her at the door. The illumination from the kitchen revealed him to her slowly, as though her senses would go into overload if she were presented with his entire presence at once.

"Rafe," she whispered to herself, trying to come to grips with his unexpected presence. She cleared her throat. "Ranger, that's enough!" she said firmly. The dog stopped barking, but continued to growl. She opened the door and motioned for Rafe to come inside. Her heart felt as though it was going to jump out of her chest.

As he moved into the light she saw his boots first—working boots that should have been retired years before. The light moved up his frame, slowly revealing him to her. Faded denim jeans lovingly clung to his long, muscular legs and emphasized his masculinity. A faded denim shirt that looked strained across his broad chest was open at the neck to reveal a strong column of dark skin at the throat. She saw a well-defined jawline bristling with a couple of days' growth of beard.

He definitely needed a haircut, she thought, noticing how his dark hair fell across his forehead to his brows. The last to be revealed as he stepped past her into the house was the expression in his black eyes.

She shivered. "What are you doing here?"

A glint of white showed when his lips turned up in a half smile. "I didn't intend to frighten you. I'm looking for Dan."

"Dan?"

"Yeah. He asked me to come back."

She placed her hand on Ranger's head. "Enough," she said to the rumbling dog. "You've made your point." She spoke without taking her eyes off Rafe.

The light mercilessly showed her that the man before her was no longer the boy she remembered. There were creases in his cheeks that bracketed his mouth. More creases covered his forehead. Deep lines were around his eyes. Whatever he'd been doing since she'd last seen him, Rafe's life hadn't been easy.

The shock of being awakened from a sound sleep to find Rafe McClain had suddenly leaped back into her life had her reeling. "How did you get here?" she asked. What she really wanted to know was if this was some stress-induced dream she was having. Could she find a way to wake up and discover she was still tucked in bed with only Ranger for company?

He leaned back against the door and allowed Ranger to check him out. When the dog appeared to be satisfied, he said, "The usual way. Plane and car—until I got to the ranch. Then I had to hoof it the rest of the way. Why does Dan have the gate padlocked? Does that have something to do with why he sent for me?"

She shook her head, trying to clear it. None of this was making any sense.

Rafe McClain was back in Texas. He was here because of Dan.

Dan. She shivered. "When did you talk to him?" she asked.

"I haven't. He wrote me a letter a while back. It took some time to catch up with me. Said he needed my help." He shrugged his shoulders. "So I'm here."

She spun away from him, needing some space from the roiling emotions he provoked within her. Peering out the window, she said, "I don't understand how you reached the house without someone seeing you."

"I didn't figure getting myself shot was part of the deal. So I was careful." He stretched and smothered a yawn.

She forced herself to face him. She leaned against the kitchen cabinet and asked, "Where have you been? I mean, where were you when Dan's letter caught up with you?"

"The Ukraine."

That surprised her, although she wasn't sure why. "What were you doing there?"

He lifted one of his eyebrows into a quirk. "You writing a book or something?"

Some things never changed. Rafe had always had a sarcastic comeback when he didn't want to answer personal questions. As far as he was concerned, every question was personal.

Why hadn't Dan ever mentioned to her that he was in touch with Rafe? The man's name had never come up in all of these years. Now she finds out Dan had contacted Rafe. Why would he have thought Rafe could help him? So many unanswered questions. They continued to race around her head.

She had to make a decision. Did she call the foreman and have Rafe evicted from the place? Surely she wasn't expected to welcome him, despite the fact that the ranch belonged to Dan, who appeared to have invited him.

Rafe drew up one of the kitchen chairs and sat down with a sigh. Mandy knew she was being rude. She could feel the hated color creep across her throat and cheeks.

She'd often envied Rafe his beautifully tanned skin that darkened into a burnished copper in the summer. In the sun she turned an angry red and peeled. She'd long since decided she needed to stay in the shade. There was nothing she could do about her thin skin that reflected her embarrassment at the most inopportune times.

This was one of them.

He must have recognized her discomfort because he decided to answer one of her questions. "I'm a consultant."

A consultant. Somehow she had trouble seeing him in a suit and tie working for a corporation.

"What kind?"

His white smile flashed across his dark face. "Believe me, you don't want to know." He looked around the room. "I like the way this place has been updated."

"So do I. Dan had it redone a couple of years ago."

"Do you live here now?"

She paused. "No. I live in Dallas. I've taken some time off."

He glanced at her hands and she realized that she was clenching them tightly. She deliberately placed them behind her and leaned against them and the cabinet.

"You're not married?" he asked, sounding surprised.

She shook her head without quite meeting his gaze. "No."

"Why not?"

It was all right for him to ask personal questions, she noticed. "Why aren't *you* married?" she replied, carrying the inquisition into his corner.

"I never stayed in one place long enough, I guess. Most women I've met tend to want their husband at home with them."

She couldn't imagine Rafe in the role of husband. He was too untamed. "I suppose," she murmured, wishing she knew what to do with him now that he was there.

"So what's your excuse?"

Her gaze darted to his. She raised her chin. "Maybe no one has asked me," she replied evenly.

He grinned and her stomach did a somersault. "I don't buy that one," he said, his gaze sliding over her in an intimate perusal that made her shiver in response.

She lifted her shoulder in a shrug. "No one that I wanted to marry, anyway." She straightened and crossed her arms over her chest. "Dan says I have lousy taste in men."

Their gazes met and held for a long, silent moment before each looked away.

"You never told me where Dan is," he said.

"He—he isn't here right now."

"Well, where in the hell is he, damn it? You keep avoiding my questions. I came a long way to find out why the hell Dan needed me here. So where is he?"

She had known that she was going to have to answer his questions and had hoped that she could talk about Dan without breaking down. But the lateness of the hour and her sense of vulnerability where Rafe was concerned weren't helping her deal with the situation.

She attempted to swallow around the lump in her throat. It was hard to put her thoughts into words. She wanted so much to be wrong.

"I think Dan's dead," she said, her voice breaking on the last word.

Two

Rafe studied the woman before him. She no doubt believed what she was saying, but it had no meaning to him. None at all.

"Dead?"

He repeated the word as though he'd never heard it before. He shook his head. "He can't be. I'd know it if something had happened to Dan. He…" His voice trailed away. He knew how stupid that sounded. He, better than most, knew how easily a life could be snuffed out. Rafe wiped a hand across his face, ignoring his exhaustion. "You'd better start at the beginning, Mandy, and fill me in on what the hell's going on around here."

Mandy picked up a glass and absently filled it with water. He thought about asking her for a drink, then decided against it. At the moment he had more important things on his mind. She faced him once again, but her lustrous gray eyes stared past his shoulder and he knew she no longer saw him sitting there.

While he waited, he looked for the young girl he'd known in the woman standing before him. There were traces of her in the way she stood, the way she moved. He still had the same strong reaction to her, he was sorry to discover.

Although she was still slender, she'd added curves that would make any man take a second look. Her satiny smooth skin made his palms itch, wanting to touch her cheek. She still wore her reddish-brown hair long. Tousled waves tumbled around her shoulders, unnecessarily reminding him that she'd just come from her warm bed.

She focused on him once more and swallowed painfully. He found her nervousness around him troubling, but he wasn't surprised.

"I haven't seen Dan in a couple of months. We've both been busy, although he usually calls me every week or so. About ten days ago I received a call from Dan's foreman, Tom Parker. He asked me if I'd seen or spoken to Dan."

"Why would he call you?"

"Because he said he'd checked with everyone else—including Dan's business partner—to see why Dan had left without letting anyone know."

"You mean he just disappeared?"

"Tom said he spoke to Dan late one afternoon. He told Dan he needed to talk to him about moving some of the cattle to a different feeding area. Dan told him he had a meeting that night, but would meet with him the next morning. However, the next morning Dan wasn't to be found."

"Does anyone know who he was meeting or where?"

"Unfortunately, no. I think he must have met someone at the airstrip and left, because his car is still in the garage and Tom found the Jeep parked at the airstrip."

"What airstrip?"

"Dan had one built on the ranch about three years ago. He and his partner were thinking of buying a plane together. According to the partner, they never did, but they rent planes from time to time and use the strip on a regular basis.''

Rafe shook his head. "This is all a jumble to me. I guess I'm going to have to get some sleep before I can make any sense of it.''

"I hope sleep helps. It hasn't helped me, although I have to admit I haven't been sleeping too well since Tom called me. I came down immediately to see if I could help figure out where he'd gone. I'm so frustrated because outside of Tom and me, no one seems to be concerned—not Dan's partner nor the sheriff's department. His partner said that Dan would be back in his own good time. I don't believe that. I don't believe that Dan would just disappear like that, especially after arranging to meet with Tom. I also think he would have called someone if he ran into some kind of a delay so that we wouldn't worry.''

"So do I. Dan is one of the most responsible people I know.''

"Exactly.'' She studied him for a moment. "You're right, Rafe. You need to get some sleep. You're out on your feet. Go on to bed. We'll discuss this in the morning.''

He knew that she was right. He could feel weariness claim his body now that he'd finally reached his destination. He stood and stepped away from the chair. "He's been missing this long. I don't suppose another few hours will matter.''

She entered the hallway and spoke as she moved away from him. "You can sleep in Dan's room.''

Rafe waited until a light turned on in the hall before he turned off the kitchen light. Ranger watched him without blinking.

"I'm glad you're watching out for her,'' he said in a low voice.

Ranger didn't change expression. Rafe got the feeling that

Ranger didn't particularly care what Rafe might think about anything.

Smart dog.

Rafe followed Mandy into the hallway.

"Dan moved into the master bedroom after Mom died," she said, motioning to the end of the hall.

Rafe paused beside her. "I was sorry to hear about your mother, Mandy. She was always kind to me. I've never forgotten that."

"It was quick," she replied, her gaze on her arms, folded across her chest. "At least she didn't suffer."

"Her heart?"

"Yes." She looked up at him. "Dad, on the other hand, lingered months longer than expected with his cancer."

He didn't want to talk about her father, not now, not ever. He stepped past her and entered one of the few rooms in this house he'd never been in before. Mandy followed him into the room and glanced into the adjoining bathroom. "There are plenty of clean towels and things," she said. "I'll talk to you in the morning."

With that, she quietly left the room, closing the door behind her.

Only then did Rafe remember that his bag was still hidden outside, but he wasn't about to go back out there tonight to look for it. He glanced around the large room. A king-size bed was on one wall. Another wall was lined with bookshelves, filled with a mishmash of fiction and nonfiction. He smiled, thinking of Dan and his love of reading.

His smiled faded when he remembered what Mandy had told him. Dan couldn't be dead. There was no way Dan would allow himself to get into a situation that was life-threatening. But accidents happened all the time, Rafe reminded himself.

Where was he? If Dan was alive, why hadn't he returned?

Rafe walked over to the third wall, next to the door leading to the bathroom. This wall was filled with photographs, large and small, of varied subjects. Most of the photos had been taken at the ranch. There were shots of longhorn cattle, deer, family pets, and many pictures of family members.

Rafe was surprised to see that he was in many of them. He hadn't remembered being that thin, or looking so grim.

As he turned away, he paused and looked again at photographs that must have been taken at the party the Crenshaws gave the night that he and Dan graduated from high school, the last night he was on the ranch.

There was a picture of Mandy in a cotton-candy-colored dress with a full skirt and sleeves that rested just off her shoulders. He still recalled, without the need of a photograph to remind him, how she looked at the party with her glowing eyes and her contagious smile. She'd looked much older than fifteen that night and had delighted in her new-found ability to attract admiring gazes. He touched the photograph lightly with his forefinger, tracing the curve of her lips, the shape of her shoulders.

He could still remember how her mouth had tasted, how smooth her shoulders had felt, how much he'd wanted to make love to her that night.

Rafe deliberately withdrew his gaze from Mandy's photo and focused instead on another one taken the day they graduated of Dan in his suit, looking solemn enough if you didn't look too closely at the amusement in his eyes. The one of Rafe alone caught him by surprise. He'd filled out from the earlier pictures Dan had on display and wore the first and only suit he'd ever possessed. Rafe looked closer at the boy he had once been. He'd had his hair cut and looked equally solemn. However, there was no amusement twinkling in his eyes, just a firm resolve to make something of himself.

He'd managed to do that, all right, with the help of Uncle Sam.

Rafe continued into the bathroom and shucked off his clothes. He stood under the hot, steamy water and let it massage the soreness from his body. He could scarcely keep his eyes open. Once the water began to cool, he turned it off and grabbed a towel. He didn't need anything to sleep in tonight. He'd raid Dan's closet in the morning so he could pick up his bag outside. Now all he wanted was a few hours of oblivion.

After Rafe closed his bedroom door, Mandy returned to bed, Ranger padding softly behind her until she turned off the light and crawled beneath the covers. Then he stretched out on the rug beside her and gave a deep sigh.

She wanted to echo that sigh.

Having Rafe McClain show up like this had been a shock she could have done without. However, now that he was here, she had to admit to herself that if anyone could solve the mystery of Dan's disappearance, it would be Rafe. She should be relieved that he had shown up. Just as important, knowing that Dan had notified his friend strengthened her belief that something in Dan's life had gone wrong. Why else would he have contacted Rafe?

Her thoughts kept circling back to the man. How could a person she hadn't seen in twelve years still have such a strong effect on her?

She would never forget the day all those years ago when he showed up at the ranch for the first time. He'd been fourteen, Dan's age. She'd been eleven.

He'd worn ragged clothes, much like what he'd had on today. He had needed a haircut, as he did now. Not much had changed in his overall appearance for that matter, she thought to herself.

He'd been thinner then. Much thinner. He'd still had bruises on his face, bruises he hadn't chosen to explain. Her mind drifted, returning to those long-ago days when she had been a child filled with curiosity, eager to learn.

Mandy was in her room on a Saturday morning, trying to decide if she was ready to pack away her dolls and other childhood things. She enjoyed playing with them once in a while, when she knew Dan wouldn't catch her at it and tease her for being such a baby. However, she could use the space they took up for other things. School started on Monday and she felt the need to organize her room and get ready to face the new school year.

It was tough being too old for toys, too young for boys.

She heard the yard dogs clamoring outside and peered out her window to see what had set them off. She saw a tall, skinny boy standing beside the gate of the fence that protected the lawn from the rest of the ranch. He stood as still as a statue, while the dogs carried on all around him.

Dan's voice carried ahead of him as he dashed out the back door, the screen slamming behind him. "Hey, Rafe! How ya doing?" Dan chased the dogs off and invited the boy inside the stone fence.

Mandy vaguely recognized the boy. He'd gone to the same elementary school in Wimberley that she and Dan had attended. Of course now the two boys would be starting high school this fall. Except maybe Rafe had dropped out of school a couple of years ago. Either that, or his family had moved away. She hadn't seen him in a long time.

Now he was back. Curious—as usual—Mandy raced downstairs and walked out on the porch. She was surprised by what he said.

"I'm looking for work."

Dan laughed. "You serious? Aren't you going to school?"

"I intend to enroll on Monday, but I need a local address.

So I thought maybe I could work here on the ranch for your dad evenings and weekends until I finish up with school.''

Dan reached over and touched a gash just above Rafe's eye and Rafe flinched. ''What happened?''

''It doesn't matter.''

''Your dad?''

''Forget it.''

''Are your folks still living in East Texas?''

''Yeah.''

''Do they know where you are?''

''No.'' He frowned at Dan. ''You gonna tell 'em?''

''Not if you don't want me to. Won't they be looking for you?''

Rafe laughed, but he didn't sound amused. ''Not hardly.'' Rafe looked past Dan and saw her watching them. He looked away. Dan turned around and saw her.

''Quit being so nosy and go back into the house,'' he yelled.

Without a word Mandy went back inside. She went looking for her mom and found her in the front yard, working in her flower garden as usual.

''Mom, there's a guy here wanting a job.''

Her mother sat back on her heels and looked quizzically at Mandy from beneath her wide-brimmed straw hat. ''Why are you telling *me,* honey? Your dad handles that.''

''He's just a kid.''

Her mother grinned. ''Really? How old is he?''

''Dan's age. They used to be in the same class until Rafe moved away or something.''

''Rafe?''

''That's what he goes by.''

Her mom got up, dusted her knees, removed her cotton gardening gloves, straightened her hat and walked around the house. She saw the boys sitting on the back steps and joined them.

Mandy followed her, daring Dan to say anything about her presence.

"Hello. I'm Dan's mother, Amelia Crenshaw," she said, holding out her hand to Rafe. Mandy noticed that her mother acted as though there was nothing unusual about his appearance.

He looked at her hand uncertainly, then reluctantly took it, shook it quickly and released it. He bobbed his head without meeting her gaze. "Hi. I'm Rafe McClain."

"Amanda tells me that you're looking for work. Is that right?"

Dan glared at Mandy. She gave him a sunny smile in return.

Rafe cleared his throat. "Yes, ma'am."

"After school, of course."

"Yes'm."

She smiled. "Why don't you come inside and have something to drink? Dan's father should be coming in for dinner in an hour or so. You can join us and discuss the matter with him."

Mandy sensed Rafe's embarrassment. He kept looking at everything but her mom. "That's all right," he mumbled. "I can come back later."

"Nonsense," her mother said gently, smiling at him. "You have to eat like the rest of us. Dan can show you around the place after you get something to drink." She walked up the steps and across the porch as though there was no doubt in her mind the boys would follow her into the house.

"Snitch," Dan muttered, walking past Mandy and pulling her hair.

"What's so secret about wanting a job?" she asked him, swatting at his hand.

Rafe glanced at her and smiled. "Nothing. There's nothing wrong.'' She smiled back, liking the boy with the black, sad eyes.

Later, over the noon meal, her dad asked Rafe a bunch of questions about what he was trained to do, but nothing about why he needed a job and a place to stay. Mandy had a hunch Dan had already filled him in on that part when she wasn't around.

And so it was that Rafe McClain made his home on the ranch on that day in late August. There was a small cabin—really only a large room with a bathroom added off the side—that was just over a rise from the house and barns. A small creek ran nearby and the place was shaded with large—and obviously old—live oak trees.

Her dad had suggested that Rafe move in there.

Nobody talked about the fact that he didn't have any belongings. He just showed up at mealtimes wearing some of Dan's old shirts and jeans. Her dad insisted on paying him in addition to his room and board—and gradually Rafe acquired a pair of shoes that weren't falling apart and had his hair cut. He worked from dawn until time for school, then from after school to dark or later.

Sometime during the following four years, Mandy developed a crush on Rafe. She could still remember the pangs of adolescent angst where he was concerned. He, on the other hand, hadn't known she existed as anything but Dan's pesky little sister.

Too bad she hadn't left things that way. Life would have been so much better for both of them if she had.

The sounds of voices and the routine of activity around a working ranch roused Rafe the next morning. He opened his eyes and lay there, remembering why he was back in Texas. He sat up and groaned, feeling the stiffness in all his joints.

He forced himself out of bed and stalked over to the

dresser in search of some briefs. When he pulled the drawers open, he let out a silent whistle. These were not discount store items. He picked up a pair of silk boxer shorts and smiled. The kid certainly believed in his comfort. He'd have to give Dan a rough time the next time he saw him.

If he saw him.

Damn. He hated the not knowing. He opened the closet door and stepped inside a spacious walk-in area. Racks of suits, dress shirts and shiny shoes were on one side. Jeans, Western-cut shirts and boots were on the other.

Interesting. It looked to Rafe like a town and country wardrobe to fit any occasion.

He tried to remember the last time he'd talked to Dan, or heard from him before this letter that had finally caught up with him. He'd gotten a short letter a couple of years ago mentioning an engagement and that he expected Rafe to show up and be his best man.

Before Rafe had found the time to respond—and he'd put it off, admittedly, because he didn't know how to remind his old friend that he wouldn't be welcome around the Crenshaw family—Dan had written an equally terse letter saying the engagement was off.

What Dan hadn't told him now spoke volumes. What did he do that called for suits, dress shirts and a wide assortment of expensive ties?

Rafe pulled one of the work shirts off a hanger and put it on. The fit was fine. He didn't have as much luck with the jeans. It seemed as though Dan had put on a little weight around the middle since high school. Rafe rooted around until he found an old pair of jeans that would fit him.

They were worn white at the knees and the seat of the pants. Hell, for all he knew they may well *be* jeans from high school.

He grabbed a pair of socks before putting on his own

boots. Then he went in search of some coffee with which to start his day.

There was no sign of Mandy but she'd left evidence of her passing. A pan of biscuits sat next to a plate filled with crisply fried bacon. He couldn't remember the last time he'd eaten. His stomach growled at the thought. He poured himself a cup of coffee and stuck a piece of bacon between two halves of a biscuit. By the time he'd finished his coffee, he'd made a large dent in the biscuit and bacon supply.

He peered outside, but there was no sign of Mandy. One of the first things he needed to do was to get his clothes out of the brush where he'd hidden them. After that, he'd talk to someone about getting his car back to the rental place. He walked to the back door and eased it open. In addition, he wanted to hunt up the foreman and get his view on what might have taken place here the night Dan disappeared.

He stepped off the end of the porch and started toward the gate. He was almost there when a slight noise at his back caused him to glance around, but he was too late. He felt a blinding pain directly behind his ear.

His last memory was a vision of the limestone walk rapidly coming up to meet him.

Three

———

Rafe knew that he was getting too old for this business if someone could take him out in a friend's backyard in the middle of the morning. He sat in the kitchen holding a cold compress to the back of his head while Mandy apologized to him and explained to the foreman that he wasn't an interloper and shouldn't have been ambushed.

From what Rafe could gather as he sat nursing his goose egg and bruised ego, Tom Parker wasn't any too pleased with Mandy's explanations. He appeared to be upset that all of his carefully planned security measures hadn't prevented Rafe from reaching the ranch house undetected last night.

At the moment, Rafe was having some difficulty working up much sympathy for the man.

"I'd intended to introduce Rafe to you this morning, Tom," Mandy said in a conciliatory tone that wasn't improving Rafe's mood of the moment. Hell, she didn't need to apologize for him. "I wasn't aware he was awake or I would have invited you to the house for coffee so the two of you could get acquainted.''

"So introduce us," the man replied in a gruff voice.

Mandy rolled her eyes. "Rafe McClain, this is Dan's foreman, Tom Parker. He's worked for Dan for several years." To Tom she added, "Rafe is a family friend."

Rafe wasn't in the mood to be polite, damn it. Getting his head bashed in wasn't on the top of his list of ways to start the day. Hell, Ranger had been better protection for Mandy than all the armed guards. Where was this character last night when Ranger had carried on so loudly?

Rafe leaned back in his chair and looked over the man who was propped against the cabinets with his arms folded, glaring at him from across the room. He wasn't particularly impressed with the man or his glare, although he might have been more tolerant of the man's attitude if this was the first time they'd had occasion to meet.

"A little quick to take a person out, aren't you?" Rafe drawled, holding Parker's gaze with a steady look.

"You're a stranger on the property. As far as I'm concerned, you have no business being here. I have zero tolerance these days."

Rafe carefully touched the knot behind his ear. "Yeah. I noticed."

"Hope you're not waiting for an apology," Parker growled. "With Dan missing, I'm not willing to take any chances where Mandy's safety is concerned."

Mandy interrupted. "Tom, I've already explained that…"

Parker ran his hand through his hair in a frustrated gesture. "Hell, I know what you said, Mandy. Has it occurred to you that if this guy—"

"Rafe—" Rafe reminded him softly.

"—If *Rafe* could get on the property without any of us seeing him, so could anyone else. Until we locate Dan, we don't know what the hell is going on. For all we know, this guy could have something to do with Dan's disappearance.''

Rafe chuckled, then groaned, holding his head very carefully, afraid it might tumble off his shoulders at any moment. ''I'm not up to laughing at your absurd accusations just yet, so try to hold back on the humor for a little while, okay?''

He was amused to see that this Tom character was actually grinding his teeth. I bet his dentist was going to love him for that.

Parker straightened. ''I've got to get to work. I need to—''

''—show me around the place?'' Rafe inserted. ''Thanks, I'd appreciate it. Now that I'm here, I can relieve you of some of the burden of figuring out what's going on.''

A rush of emotions seemed to sweep across Parker's face—disbelief, anger, with more than a hint of bewilderment. ''Just who in the hell do you think you are?'' he finally managed to get out through clenched teeth.

Rafe continued to lean back in his chair. He smiled, feeling better by the minute. ''The man who's going to find out what happened to Dan.''

''I see. You think you can do any better than I have, or Mandy, or the sheriff's department?''

Rafe shrugged. ''Won't know 'til I try.''

Mandy spoke up. ''Look, Rafe, you don't have to stay. Just because Dan contacted you doesn't mean that you have to—''

''Dan contacted him! When?'' Parker turned and looked at Rafe. ''How come I've never heard of you, if you're such good friends with the family?''

Rafe scratched his chin thoughtfully. ''Tell you what, Parker,'' he finally drawled. ''The minute I finish my autobiography, I'll make damned sure you get the first copy off the press. Until then, I don't owe you any explanations about anything, you understand me? I'm here now. I aim to stay until I get ready to leave, and not one minute sooner.'' He studied the other man thoughtfully before adding, ''Unless you're already seeing yourself as the boss around here now that Dan isn't around.''

Parker straightened and took a step toward him before Mandy stepped in front of him. She placed her hands on Parker's chest. ''Look, Tom, I know Rafe very well. You aren't going to win this argument. I'll talk to him...try to get him to calm down—''

''Calm down?'' Rafe repeated. ''Hell, Mandy, if I was any more calm at the moment, I'd be comatose.''

She ignored him. ''Why don't you give us a few minutes,'' she said to Parker. ''Rafe and I will be out later. I want to show him the airfield and other things that weren't here the last time he was here. I'd like you to go with us.''

Rafe idly noted that Parker contented himself by giving Rafe a hard look. Rafe assumed it was supposed to make him tremble in his boots. Parker nodded to Mandy and left the kitchen, allowing the door to slam behind him.

''His mother must not have taught him much manners, slamming the door that way,'' Rafe commented. He got up and went over to the coffeepot and carefully poured himself another cup. His head hurt something fierce, but he'd be hanged before he'd admit his pain to Mandy.

Part of the macho creed, he supposed, amused at himself.

''Oh, you're a great one to be spouting off about manners. You practically accused him of doing away with Dan so he could run the ranch!'' Mandy turned away and quickly scrambled some eggs and placed them on a plate along with what was left of the bacon and biscuits. She set the plate hard enough down at the table where he'd been sitting that Rafe feared for the safety of the china plate.

''Eat,'' she said tersely.

''What about you?''

"I've managed to look after myself just fine for all these years without your help, McClain. I don't need you or any other man looking after me, have you got that straight?"

"Look, Mandy, I'm not sure why you're upset, but I—" But he what? Was he sorry for anything he'd said or done? Not only no, but hell no. So what did he say to her? "I don't want to see you upset," he finally muttered.

"Then sit down and eat your breakfast," was her only reply.

He sat down and ate his breakfast, which he found a little tough to do since he'd already helped himself to a large portion earlier. But he figured it wouldn't hurt to pacify her at the moment. She seemed to be just a mite touchy. Maybe he should have taken into consideration all she'd been through these past few days before he let loose at the foreman.

"You had no reason to accuse Tom of trying to take over the ranch," she finally said from across the room, where she busied herself loading the dishwasher. He tried not to wince when breakables collided.

"Didn't I? Well, that's good to hear."

"He and Dan are very close."

"So?"

"If you think that he might have had anything to do with Dan's disappearance—"

"Whoa! Now wait a minute, Mandy. That's quite a leap you've made between the two subjects."

"Is it? I don't think so. You're implying that Tom has something to gain if we can't find Dan."

"Am I? Funny, but I don't see it that way. In the first place, I don't know enough about what has happened to start coming up with conclusions about anything."

"Then what were you implying by your out-of-line comment?"

He grinned. "I figure he was making damned sure that I

understood he'd already staked his claim where you're concerned and he didn't like the idea I might be trespassing on that claim.''

''Me?!''

''Aw, come on, Mandy. You're not that naive. The man is obviously playing the protector role where you're concerned. Not that I blame him. In his place I'd be doing the same thing. After all, if Dan hadn't been worried about something several weeks ago, he never would have sent me that letter. The fact that he has now disappeared and no one seems to know why or where, or even—God forbid!—if he's even alive tells me we've got something serious on our hands. If something *has* happened to Dan, that leaves you in a very vulnerable position.''

She stopped what she was doing and looked at him. ''In what way?''

''You're a very attractive woman, Mandy, as well as being the only family member left to inherit the ranch if something *has* happened to Dan. Don't pretend not to see what a sweet setup that would be for some unscrupulous male.''

''Ah. I see. You think Tom hopes to acquire me and this ranch in one neat package. How gracious of you to believe that a man would want more than just me in a relationship. Not only that, you've already managed to figure out that Tom is just unscrupulous enough to make a play for me based on those terms.'' She crossed her arms and glared at him from across the room. ''What sort of stuff are you smoking these days, Rafe? I swear, you must be downright delusional!''

He certainly wasn't making any points at the moment, Rafe decided. So maybe he'd better get started on his plans for the day.

He got up and carried his dishes to where she stood. Nudging her aside, he rinsed his plate, utensils, cup and saucer and quietly placed them in the dishwasher. He looked down at her, suddenly amused at the fiery glints shooting from her eyes. He'd forgotten how much fun he'd had as a kid teasing her in order to provoke just that expression.

He had a sudden urge to kiss her, just to provoke another reaction. He leaned toward her, wondering if she would taste as sweet as he remembered. She'd been staring past him, looking out the window. When he leaned toward her, she glanced back, focusing on him once again.

Their eyes met and he realized how much trouble he'd be in if he actually followed through on the idea. Man, what was he thinking!

He immediately straightened and turned away. He had already learned one thing since he'd returned to Texas. Mandy Crenshaw affected the grown man just as strongly as she had the young boy. This time, he was supposed to have enough self-discipline not to succumb to the temptation she presented.

Four

Rafe walked over to the door and looked outside, watching the activity in the ranch yard and concentrating on why he was there. "You mentioned Dan's partner last night," he finally asked when it became obvious that Mandy wasn't going to speak. "His partner in what?"

"He and James Williams started a business with computers. I think they met in college. They make circuit boards for computer companies who want to hire that part out. I guess they've been fairly successful. I know they have a small factory with over fifteen employees. James takes care of running the plant—he's some kind of computer whiz—while Dan's been handling sales and contacting potential clients."

She walked over to the table and sat down. Rafe glanced around and saw what she had done. With a certain amount of reluctance he decided to join her. He needed whatever information Mandy could give him. The sooner he resolved the matter, the sooner he could hightail it out of there.

He crossed the room and sat down across from her. "Which would explain why he spends his time traveling," he replied, thinking out loud.

She nodded.

"But this Williams—he doesn't know where Dan could be?"

"No, but he said he isn't worried. He said Dan travels all the time. When I pinned him down, he admitted that Dan usually lets him know when he's going to be out of town for any length of time." She hugged her waist. "He's never been out of touch for this long."

"When is the last time either the foreman or Dan's partner saw him?"

"It's been almost two weeks now since July 1. Tom said he spoke to Dan that evening, but he wasn't around the next morning when he came up to the house for their meeting."

"Any of his clothes gone?"

She shrugged. "I have no way of knowing. Plenty of his things are still here. I don't know what kind of luggage he kept, so I have no way of knowing if he has bags with him."

"You mentioned last night that you reported this to the sheriff. What sort of response did you receive from that avenue?"

"A deputy came out to talk to me. He was very patronizing. Asked a lot of personal questions about me and my interest in my brother and his possible disappearance. Wanted to know if I was his heir if something had happened to him. He was a real jerk."

"Do you remember the deputy's name?"

"Oh, yeah. I'd never forget it. Dudley Wright. I think of him as Dudley DoRight. Treated me like some kind of neurotic female who needed to get a life instead of trailing along behind my brother, asking inane questions." She looked at Rafe for what seemed to be a long time before she asked, "Do you think there's a chance Dan could still be alive?"

"Will you stop thinking that way?" Rafe replied in a growl. "Just because we don't know where he is doesn't mean he's dead. There could be all sorts of explanations why we haven't heard from him. Let's don't start jumping to conclusions."

"Then why hasn't he been in touch with anyone?" she replied with some heat. "Why is it I'm the only one who sees something strange about the fact that he hasn't gotten in touch with me, or with Tom, or even James?"

He shook his head as though he wasn't sure what she was implying. "You think it's a conspiracy?" he finally asked. "You think everyone else knows where he is but no one is telling you?"

She glared at him. "Oh, puleeze. So now you're agreeing with the good deputy and think I'm neurotic as well?"

Rafe took a deep breath and let it out very slowly. "For what it's worth, Mandy, I think you're a tad sensitive about what others might or might not think of you. Like you, I'm puzzled about how a person could disappear like that without somebody, somewhere, knowing what happened and where he is now. It's possible someone knows more than he or she realizes he knows." He rearranged the salt and pepper shaker, moving them around each other. He glanced up at her. "When did you last speak to him?"

Mandy was quiet for a moment. When she spoke, she sounded calmer. "About a month ago. He'd been checking on me more often than usual. During that particular conversation he suggested that I might want to take my vacation early and come to visit him." Her voice wobbled and she swallowed before continuing. "He said we hadn't spent much time together since Mom died. He thought I could use a break."

"From what?"

She nibbled her lower lip. "I recently broke an engagement."

"Seems to run in the family." He smiled, trying to put her at ease. "Dan wrote me about his engagement. Then later let me know there was not going to be a wedding."

She shook her head. "That was Sharon. He seemed to be crazy about her. All she wanted to do was party. I wasn't sorry to see her back out of their engagement, although I think Dan took it hard at the time."

"Could his disappearance have anything to do with her?"

She looked at him, startled. "Oh, I don't think so. That was a couple of years ago. He's dated several women since then."

"Any seriously enough that they might have some idea where he would be?"

"I don't know. I could talk to James about it." She hesitated, then said, "Better yet, I'll let you talk to him. He makes me uncomfortable."

"How?"

"Every time I see him, he makes a pass at me." She shivered, as though repulsed by the idea.

Rafe smiled. "The man shows good taste, at least."

She frowned. "Very funny."

He could see he wasn't going to win any points around her at the moment. He shoved back his chair and stood. "I'm going out to get my bag. Is the cabin in use these days? If not, I might as well bunk down in it." He moved rapidly toward the door, but came to an abrupt halt when Mandy spoke.

"Uh, no. The cabin burned a few months after you left here."

He turned around.

"Really," he said softly. "How did that happen?"

She shrugged. "One of the hands got careless, was my dad's guess. Left a smoldering cigarette too close to something flammable. By the time anyone saw it, the cabin was in full blaze. It was too late to do anything but keep the fire from spreading.''

Rafe looked out the window for a moment before returning his gaze to her. ''Then I'll find a motel in town. I have a rental car parked outside the gate that I need to return. I figure there are enough vehicles around the ranch for me to use one of them while I'm here.''

''Of course you can use one of the pickup trucks and there's no reason why you can't continue to stay here at the house. Dan isn't going to mind your using his room and you know it.''

Rafe knew that he would get little rest staying in the same house with Mandy. He needed all the distance he could muster between them. However, his choices at the moment were limited. In his opinion, the ranch held the key to Dan's disappearance. It made more sense for him to stay put.

''What about Parker?'' he finally asked. ''He's not going to like us sleeping under the same roof.''

''And whose fault is that? You certainly didn't put yourself out trying to get along with him.''

''Yeah, I'm funny that way. Somebody slugs me from behind with no warning, I become very judgmental about his character.''

''You know why he did that.''

''I know why you think he did it, but I'm not buying his explanation. He could see I was making no effort to hide, for God's sake. I was no threat to any one. It's my guess he doesn't want anyone hanging around you. He might have figured that taking me out would discourage me from lingering for more than a brief visit.''

''Will you please stop it! Tom isn't interested in me...*or* in acquiring this ranch through me. Really, Rafe. I don't remember you being so cynical.''

''Right. I always waited around for the Easter bunny

every spring." He walked out the door and let the screen slam behind him. He strode across the porch shaking his head at his juvenile behavior.

What did it matter to him what kind of relationship Mandy might have with the foreman of Dan's ranch, anyway? Maybe he was still reeling from too many hours of travel. Mandy had nothing to do with the reason he was here. He needed to remember that.

"You looking for something?"

He stopped in his tracks and slowly turned around. Parker stood a few feet away, his hands on his hips. Damned if he didn't look like a gunfighter waiting to draw on him.

"I left my bag out there," he said, nodding toward the thick foliage across from the house. "Thought I'd go pick it up. You got a problem with that?"

Parker ignored his question and asked one of his own. "How long you intending to stay?"

Rafe turned back and continued to walk toward the brush, forcing Parker to follow him if he intended to continue the conversation. "Until Dan shows up. Why?"

"Then you think he's still alive."

Rafe stopped. Why in hell was everyone so willing to think that Dan was dead. "Don't you?" he asked pointedly.

Parker shifted his feet, removed his hat, smoothed his hair, replaced his hat, then looked toward the rolling hills that surrounded them. "I don't know what to think," he finally admitted. "He's never just disappeared like this before. He'd know we'd be worried about him and would do everything in his power to let us know if he was all right. If he could. I think something's happened to him. I'm just not sure what. It's been too long now. Much too long."

"Tell me about the airstrip."

Parker looked at him, surprised by the shift in subject. "What about it?"

"Can you hear when a plane lands or takes off from the ranch buildings?"

"Sometimes. When the wind's right."

"Did you hear a plane the night Dan disappeared?"

"I don't remember."

"Mandy mentioned his Jeep being found down there. I figure that's how he left the place. Which reminds me, I need to turn in my rental car. Is there someone who can follow me into Austin?"

Parker took his own sweet time about answering. "I can send Carlos," he finally said.

Rafe nodded in acknowledgment of the foreman's reluctance to accommodate him in any way. "Thanks," he said wryly. Rafe pushed through the thick undergrowth and picked up his bag. When he came out, Parker was still standing there.

"You made my efforts at security look pretty bad, coming in like you did. How did you manage to do that?"

"I'm professionally trained to get in and out of places without anyone knowing about it, courtesy of the United States government. So don't feel too bad, okay? Unless enemy infiltrators decide to take over the country by starting with this ranch, your security is just fine."

He turned away and left Parker standing there, a frown seemingly etched permanently on the man's face.

Rafe figured it probably wouldn't hurt for him to brush up a little on his people skills now that he was back in the States. He could see that he certainly wasn't winning many points around here. Then again, he had no plans to teach any Dale Carnegie courses as a second career, either.

His immediate plans were to find out what had happened to Dan.

Mandy watched Rafe slam out of the house. What was she going to do if she wasn't able to better handle her reactions to him? It was obvious that he had no intention of leaving until the mystery of Dan's disappearance was solved.

She should be feeling relief that she could turn the matter over to someone as capable as Rafe appeared to be. There was nothing to be gained by her continuing to stay on at the ranch. Her life was in Dallas, after all. She could go home, return to her job and wait there for developments.

She had come to the ranch when Tom first notified her about Dan's disappearance, thinking it would help her peace of mind to be closer to where he had disappeared. She had thought that if and when Dan did show up, he would return to the ranch. Unfortunately, now that Rafe had arrived there was no more peace of mind to be found.

This morning had certainly proven that. They couldn't be in the same room without arguing. Which was ridiculous. She generally got along with everyone, but Rafe seemed to deliberately bait her with his caustic remarks.

As if his attitude wasn't irritating enough, there had been a moment there when she'd suddenly felt as though he was about to kiss her. She'd looked up at him and seen something in his eyes that had started her heart racing. She must have imagined it, though. He'd turned away as though nothing had happened.

Oh, but something *had* happened to her. She'd been thrown back into all those confusing feelings she'd had for Rafe McClain when she'd been a teenager.

Her thoughts drifted back to that time in her life...when she had been fifteen and in love for the first time.

After weeks of feverish anticipation, the night had finally arrived for the big barbecue celebrating the high school graduation of Dan and Rafe. Mandy could scarcely contain herself. Her mother had allowed Mandy to choose the dreamiest dress she'd ever owned to wear to the party. She loved the soft pink color, but more important to her was the fact that the neckline barely hung on each shoulder, the sleeves puffing out and thereby disguising her rather bony shoulders. The dress accented her small waist, then flared in a full-skirted way to her knees, with flouncing petticoats beneath it.

Mandy took a last look at herself in the mirror before going outside. She no longer looked like a child. In this dress, she appeared to be a full-fledged woman—attractive, seductive and alluring. She leaned closer and slowly smiled at her reflection…and blinked…startled at the sensuality she portrayed. Wow, she scarcely knew herself.

She patted her hair, swept up in a coil with an ornamental comb, blew herself a kiss and strolled out of her room.

She paused once she reached the patio. There had never been a more beautiful Texas night, she decided. The stars looked as though they'd been freshly polished and hung, glittering on the black velvet backdrop of sky.

She breathed deeply and smiled. The giant barbecue smoker had been going long enough that the scent permeated the area.

A large dance floor had been laid down on the back lawn, surrounded by the live oak trees that shaded the house and surrounding area from the blazing Texas sun. Lines of Chinese lanterns stretched from tree to tree, casting colorful lights and adding a festive atmosphere.

People would soon be arriving, bringing casseroles, salads and desserts. Her mom and dad had been planning this party for weeks. Their friends, neighbors and all the members of the graduating class and their families were invited. Her dad was in charge of seeing there was enough barbecued brisket, ribs and chicken for everyone.

Mandy wondered if her folks would do this again in another two years when *she* graduated. If so, she hoped that Dan and Rafe would be there to help her celebrate.

Rafe had mentioned the possibility of his going into the military sometime this summer, but Dan wanted him to stay at the ranch and go to college. Dan had talked about possible scholarships that were available. Rafe would certainly qualify because his grades were excellent.

Mandy didn't want Rafe to leave. Her dad had promised her that as soon as she turned sixteen he would allow her to go on single dates. He was still living in the Stone Age, insisting that she could only go out with a group until that time, preferably one that included Dan. Neither she nor Dan liked that idea at all. But once she was sixteen, she hoped that Rafe would ask her out on a date.

Of course he had no idea how she felt about him. She'd made sure that no one did. If Dan got a hint that she had a crush on Rafe, he would never let her forget it. He'd taunt and embarrass her every chance he got.

People would be arriving any minute, but for now it was just her parents and the hands making sure there were enough tables, chairs and picnic tables outside for people to have a place to sit and eat.

Mandy wandered away from the lights so that she could enjoy the luminous heavens. She loved living on the ranch away from the city lights. It gave her a sense of belonging to the land that she had never felt whenever she visited anywhere else.

From her sheltered position, Mandy spotted Dan and Rafe when they came out of the house. They looked so grown up in their Western-styled summer suits. She'd never seen Rafe dressed so formally. He'd chosen a light beige, which set off his bronzed skin tones. Rafe and Dan were opposites in coloring, opposites in personality, but were as close as brothers, closer, even, because they never really quarreled.

Dan had been the team quarterback for the past two years. Because of the extra time it took for him to practice and play, Rafe had covered for him here at the ranch, doing the work they'd both been assigned without complaint.

Rafe showed no interest in sports. He'd always been a loner and seemed to prefer his own company even when he was on the ranch. He probably wouldn't have come to the party if her mother hadn't insisted that the party was for both of them.

A couple of hours later Mandy found herself on the dance floor, having the time of her life. It must be the dress. All of Dan's classmates seemed to suddenly discover her to-night and were giving her the rush.

She loved the attention. She hoped Rafe had noticed.

When she looked around for him, she saw him standing with her dad and some of his friends, listening to them talk. With newfound courage, Mandy walked up to him and in front of her dad and everyone else said, "When are you going to dance with me, Rafe?"

His ears reddened and one of the men chuckled, causing Rafe to stiffen slightly. "How about now?" he replied in a husky voice.

He held out his hand.

Mandy couldn't believe it. He was actually going to dance with her. She almost laughed out loud, but that wouldn't do. She smiled, the smile she'd been practicing in front of the mirror, and grasped his hand.

He felt warm, which wasn't surprising. Even though it was after ten o'clock, it was probably still eighty degrees outside. He looked as if he'd like nothing more than to remove his Western string tie, unbutton his collar and toss aside his jacket.

That was the first thing she asked him when they started to dance to the slow, melodious music from the tape deck that had been set up for the party.

"Why don't you get comfortable? It's too hot for a jacket."

He glanced around at the other males, young and old, dancing nearby. "I don't know. I guess I thought I was supposed to wear it all evening."

"Naw. Dan had his off fifteen minutes after the party started."

He smiled. "You look cool enough, like cotton candy."

"Yuck. That stuff is so sticky it gets all over you."

"I was thinking about your bared shoulders. That dress makes you look years older."

Ah, bless him. What a wonderful thing for her to hear. "Thank you." She took a breath, then blurted out, "I think you look very handsome in your suit, Rafe. I've never seen you in one before."

"That's for sure. And I doubt you'll ever see me in another one." He reached up and unbuttoned his collar. "I feel like I'm in a straitjacket."

"Then you sure don't want to go into the Army. They always have to dress up like that."

"Good point. Actually, it looks like I'm going to be staying here after all. After Dan nagged me into it, I applied to Southwest Texas State University in San Marcos earlier this spring. I didn't tell anyone because I wasn't sure if they'd take me or not. I just found out that I've been accepted. It's close enough that I could continue to work and live on the ranch. There are a couple of scholarships that are going to pay for books and tuition for the first semester. We'll see how I do after that, but at least it's a start."

"Oh, Rafe, that's wonderful. I'm so proud of you!"

His grin flashed in his dark face. He smiled so seldom that she felt a pleasurable rush to be able to witness it now. "Well, it's not exactly Harvard, but it's a fine school and I'm looking forward to it."

"I think Dan is so dumb, wanting to go to Harvard. He should be going to Texas A & M. After all, he's going to be running this ranch someday. He should be learning how to do that instead of taking some silly business courses.''

"Dan knows what he wants. Besides, your dad has taught us both a great deal about ranching.''

"So maybe you'll end up being the foreman here. Wouldn't that be neat?''

"No. After I get a little more education, I want to get out and see something of the world.''

"Will you take me with you?'' she asked, feeling oh, so daring.

He laughed and swung her around the dance floor. The first song had ended and another one immediately began. She sighed, and stepped in closer to him. When he finally answered her, she was disappointed to hear him say, "I don't think you'd want to travel the way I'm planning to go about it.''

She tilted her head up slightly so that she could see his eyes. "Oh, really, and how's that?''

"I want to hop a freighter and work my passage. I want to visit different countries, learn new languages, get to know different people and their cultures.''

"I could do that, too, you know.''

"They don't let girls do that. It's too dangerous.''

"Well, maybe so, but you would be there to protect me.''

He hugged her to him. "You're so sweet. Has anyone ever told you that before?''

This close to him, she could feel his heart thudding in his chest, as though he'd been running. She liked being so close. It was as if their bodies had been designed to fit together. Rafe slid his hand down her spine to her waist, then took several fast, turning steps which she followed as though they'd been practicing together.

"You're a good dancer, Rafe,'' she whispered. "The best I've danced with tonight.''

"Believe it or not, they made us learn in gym class during

one of the semesters last year. I found out it was fun once you learned the steps.''

"When I get older, will you take me dancing in Austin and places?"

"Sure. If I'm still around."

She rested her head on his shoulder and they continued to dance together as the evening wore on. People began to drift away as the evening grew later. She heard the sound of slamming car and truck doors, engines revving up, tires throwing gravel, but none of it could spoil the mood she and Rafe had found, dancing under the Texas stars on a summer night.

Eventually her mom called her to help with the cleanup. She and Rafe pitched in, gathering trash and carrying food to the house. By the time everything was put away in the kitchen and Mandy looked for Rafe again, he was nowhere to be found.

She didn't want the night to be over. There was magic in the air and she wanted to share it with someone special. She wanted to share it with Rafe.

Mandy checked inside the house first, just in case he was there with Dan. When she didn't find him, she decided to follow the dirt track to the cabin where he lived.

He had left without telling her good-night.

He'd left without giving her a good-night kiss.

She had known that he'd wanted to kiss her while they were dancing. She also had known that he wouldn't attempt to do so in front of everyone.

How could she forget how he had looked at her, how he'd held her pressed against him, so that she felt his body as an extension of her own?

She arrived at the cabin breathless, not all of it caused by the fact that she had hurried. She knew her parents would not approve of her being there. Maybe it was wrong, but it felt right to her. There was no way she could go to bed now and expect to sleep—not without seeing Rafe first.

There was a light on inside. She smiled to herself. He was home. With more than a hint of bravado, she tapped on the door and waited expectantly.

There was a pause before she heard him say, "Who is it?"

"It's Mandy," she said, still trying to catch her breath.

In her nervousness, it seemed to take hours for him to open the door. When he did, she was surprised to see that not only had he removed his jacket and tie, but he'd also unbuttoned his shirt so that it hung open, revealing his bare chest. He stood there in the doorway barefoot, obviously getting ready for bed. At that moment Mandy knew he was the most gorgeous male creature she'd ever seen.

He stared at her in disbelief. "What are you doing here?"

"You disappeared without telling me good-night."

"Oh. Sorry. Good night." He started to close the door.

She quickly pushed it open and stepped inside. "And...I wanted to give you your graduation present from me."

He looked at her as though wondering if she'd slipped a mental cog or two. "You gave that to me this morning, Mandy. The wallet. Don't you remember?"

She smiled. "This one is a little more personal than that." She stepped closer to him and put her arms around his neck. Leaning into him, she said, "I wanted to give you a graduation kiss," she whispered, pressing her mouth against his.

His mouth felt warm and firm beneath hers. He'd caught his breath when she threw her arms around him. She wasn't sure whether out of shock or surprise. He put his hands on each side of her waist as though to push her away. But he didn't push her away at all. Instead Rafe began to kiss her back, slowly, sensuously, as though there was nothing else in his world but her, nothing else he needed to do but kiss and caress her.

All of her girlish dreams were coming true right then and there. She was finally in Rafe's arms, kissing him. What was even more wonderful to her way of thinking was that he was kissing her back.

He held her as he had during their dances, still swaying slightly. He nibbled on her ear and down her neck before returning to her lips. She could almost hear the music and feel the beat, although the strong, steady rhythm could be coming from her heart.

"Ah, Mandy, you rip me up inside," he whispered. "I want you so much and you're such an innocent. You're too young and I can't—" He groaned and kissed her again, holding her so tightly that she knew without a doubt exactly how strongly he wanted her. Instead of frightening her, the knowledge made her feel very adult. Her crush wasn't so absurd, not if her feelings were returned.

She slid her hands from around his neck and rubbed them over his bare chest. He shivered without breaking the kiss. He coaxed her with his tongue to open her mouth and she felt as though he'd taken possession of her in the true sense of the word, the kiss being a silent vow each of them made. She belonged to him.

"Mandy!"

She jerked her head toward the open doorway. She had forgotten about the door when she came in. Now her father stood there staring at them, his rage growing.

Rafe dropped his arms and stepped away from her. She realized how this must look to her father, with Rafe half dressed. She was completely clothed, but that made no difference to her father. He must have decided that Rafe's state of undress showed his intentions.

"What the hell do you think you're doing!" her father bellowed at Rafe, storming into the small cabin.

Rafe never changed expression. He looked first at Mandy, then her father. Finally he said, "Kissing your daughter."

He sounded quite calm, particularly when compared to her father, who was getting louder with each word.

"You keep your stinking hands off her, do you hear me? Is this the way you repay me for giving you a home, by seducing my daughter?"

Rafe gave her father a long, silent look before he said, "I was under the impression that I've earned everything I ever received on your ranch, Mr. Crenshaw."

"Well, if you think you've earned the right to paw my daughter, you're dead wrong. I gave you a chance to make something of yourself. That's what I gave you. You're damned lucky you haven't been living on the streets for the past four years." He looked at her. "Go home, Mandy. Your mother will want to talk to you."

Mandy knew that she had to explain, that she had to tell her father the truth—Rafe had nothing to do with her being there. Only she'd never seen her father so angry before and she was frightened. In a panic she darted out of the cabin, hoping that once he calmed down she would be able to explain to her father that Rafe hadn't invited her to his cabin. That she had come on her own.

Her attempted explanations made no difference. Rafe left the ranch that night and she never heard from nor saw him again.

Until last night.

Five

Mandy walked outside and looked around. There was no sign of Rafe but Tom was over by one of the horse corrals. She walked over to him. "Did you happen to see where Rafe went?"

Tom resettled his hat on his head before he replied, "He and Carlos went into town."

"Oh, that's right. To return the car."

"Yeah." Tom leaned on the fence and looked at her. "How well do you know this guy, anyway?"

She bristled. "What do you mean?"

"You said he was a friend of the family, but I've never heard of him and I know everyone you call friend in these parts."

"He used to live on the ranch years ago, when we were in high school."

"What's he been doing since then?"

"I have no idea."

"Then why do you trust him?"

"Because Dan does. If Dan wrote him asking him to come back, that's good enough for me."

Suspicion was written all over Tom's face. "Did you see the letter?"

She smiled. "Do you really think Rafe would lie?"

"How the hell should I know!" he said, throwing up his hands. "That's why I'm asking you. For all I know, he may have had something to do with Dan's disappearance."

Mandy nodded. "You're right. You don't know Rafe at all." She leaned against the fence next to Tom. "Rafe's the reason I now work for Children's Services. Not that he knows that, or would care if he heard it. Looking back, I'd have to say that Rafe McClain influenced my life as much if not more than any other person did. I don't think I ever really saw that until right now." She glanced over at him. "Funny how much of what we do is unconscious, isn't it?"

Tom raised his brow. "How did he have any influence over your choice of a career?"

"He came from an abusive home and ran away when he was barely fourteen. Given the chance, he worked hard both here and at school to make something of himself. I decided that I wanted to help others who, like Rafe, weren't given an even start in life." She looked back at Tom. "I know if I told him he would not be impressed. He was quite something, even back then."

"Did a little hero worship maybe get mixed up in there somewhere?"

"More than a little. I wasn't aware he and Dan had stayed in touch all this time. Dan has never mentioned him to me. Not once in all these years. If asked, I would have said that I never expected to see him again." She brushed her hair off her forehead and sighed. "It was quite a shock to me for him to show up so unexpectedly in the middle of the night like that."

"It was a shock for both of us, let me tell you. I've been sleeping easy thinking this place was protected by tight security. It didn't help matters any for me to realize I'd been kidding myself. It bothers me to know you were up there at the house with so little protection."

"Don't worry. Ranger did fine last night. He would have stopped anyone from coming in if I hadn't reassured him that Rafe was a friend. He's a good deterrent to trouble. You've trained him well."

"Yeah, too bad Dan didn't have Ranger with him that night. Things might have worked out differently."

"Let's see what Rafe comes up with, Tom. I have a hunch that if anyone can find Dan, Rafe can."

Mandy returned to the house, poured herself a cup of coffee and sat down. Somehow she was going to have to come to terms with Rafe's return before she saw him again.

She found it difficult to believe that he had shown up so suddenly in her life. The shock of seeing him had thrown her into her past to one of the most painful times in her memory.

She'd been crying when she reached the house that night. Her mother waited just inside the kitchen.

"Sit down, Amanda," she'd said, causing Mandy to cry harder. "You were at Rafe's tonight, weren't you?"

Mandy nodded. Her mother handed her a box of tissues. "You know better than that."

"We weren't doing anything wrong, Mom. Honest. I just wanted to tell him good-night and to—well, to…" How could she tell her mother that she'd wanted to kiss Rafe? Her mother was too old to understand how important Rafe was to her.

"You had no business going down there."

"And Daddy was saying su-such aw-awful things to him," she sobbed. "He was making it sound as though Rafe had done something wrong and he hasn't." Her anger began to assert itself. "He hadn't done anything. It was me who went down there...he didn't know I was going to do that."

"So you got him in trouble."

"Yes! And I didn't mean to. Now Daddy's mad at him and it's all my fa-fault." She buried her head in her arms resting on the table.

Her mother patted her shoulder. "Your father is very protective of his children. You know that. I'll talk to him when he gets back. I'm sure this will all blow over."

When Mandy discovered that Rafe had left, she was filled with guilt and shame. She'd knocked him out of a place to stay while he went to college. In the following weeks she asked Dan if he'd heard from Rafe, but he hadn't. She told him about Rafe's acceptance at the university and his need to stay on the ranch and work.

Dan had no sympathy with her. He gave her a chewing out for being so stupid and said she didn't deserve having Rafe for a friend. She wondered if Dan still felt that way. Was that why he'd never told her that he knew how to contact Rafe?

Just seeing him again brought back all her old feelings of guilt and shame. Seeing him again also forced her to look at why she had broken off her engagement, why she'd never allowed herself to become close to another man. Somewhere deep inside, she'd judged herself as undeserving of a relationship. Look what she'd done to the first male she'd ever fallen in love with—knocked him out of going to school, forced him to leave the only stable home he'd had.

Mandy rubbed her forehead. She'd had no idea that she had harbored those feelings for so many years. Intellectually she could shoot all kinds of holes in the logic, but it wasn't her intellect that had made those judgments. It was her emotions.

Without her being aware of it, she had given Rafe a great deal of power over her since that night when she was fifteen years old. Too much power. Yes, she had been wrong to visit him and place him in the position of having to defend her presence in his cabin. Yes, her father had been wrong to believe that Rafe had lured her down there for his own purposes.

Her mother had been quick to put him straight on that one! By the next morning he had gone back to the cabin to apologize for his knee-jerk reaction, but it had been too late.

Rafe disappeared that night. He didn't go to San Marcos that fall. He made no effort to contact any of them, or so she had thought. So he had made some choices of his own. He could have gone to school. He could have returned to the ranch and faced her father with the truth of what happened once her father had calmed down.

She sighed. She'd had enough on her mind worrying about Dan. Now she was going to have to deal with Rafe. She felt like being a coward and running back to Dallas to wait for news of Dan.

Mandy reminded herself that she was no longer fifteen years old. She was an adult and would have to deal with the situation she found herself in. However, she didn't have to like it.

Rafe returned to the ranch mid-afternoon and went looking for Tom. Instead, he found Mandy.

"I was waiting for you," she said, when he found her in the barn. "I'll take you to the airstrip in the Jeep now, if you'd like."

"Where's Tom?"

In a flat tone Mandy replied, "After your warm and friendly treatment of him this morning, Tom had a tough time forcing himself to get on with the work he'd scheduled for today rather than wait for you to show up. I know he was looking forward to an afternoon of bonding with you, no doubt certain the two of you were going to end up being best friends.''

He studied her for a couple of minutes in silence. ''Funny, but I don't remember your being quite this sarcastic when you were growing up.''

''I'm surprised you remember me at all,'' she said, glancing around the barn before meeting his eyes.

''Uh-huh.'' The look he gave her made her drop her gaze. She knew her cheeks were turning red. ''Let's go,'' she said, motioning to the Jeep. He walked over to the driver's side and crawled in. Why didn't it surprise her that he chose to drive? Rafe was definitely a man determined to be in control of his environment.

Mandy figured it was up to her to let him know he wasn't in charge of her. However, she intended to choose her battles, and driving the Jeep wasn't even a respectable skirmish.

She spoke only to give him directions. He didn't speak at all. Instead he studied the terrain around them as he drove. The path to the airstrip was well-worn, which surprised Mandy. She had no idea that Dan spent much time out here.

When they reached the area, Rafe pulled over and parked beneath the shade of one of the large trees that dotted the range. He turned off the engine but didn't move to get out. Mandy remained in the bucket seat beside him, listening to the ticking sounds made by the hot engine cooling off. She was determined to ignore the heat.

There was very little breeze moving across the land. The temperatures were flirting with the hundred-degree mark. Nothing was stirring. Besides the lack of shade, Mandy knew that Dan didn't allow any of the cattle loose in this pasture because of the airstrip.

''How long has this been here?'' Rafe finally asked, breaking the somnolent silence between them.

''About four years, I think.''

"Why?"

"Why did he build it? Originally it was because he intended to buy a plane. But when he and James looked into the upkeep of one, plus the need to build a hangar to protect it, they chose to rent whenever they needed one."

"I need to talk to this Williams guy to find out what he knows."

"Good luck. There's no doubt you'll have more luck than I did if he'll talk to you at all. He made light of all my questions."

All the while they spoke, Rafe surveyed the area. "I've never been to this part of the ranch before. As I recall, your dad didn't use it much."

"No. Dad never liked to run cattle in here because of the breaks and hollows in the land back over there." She nodded with her chin. "They were too hard to get to if any of them wandered into those arroyos."

"This is where you found the Jeep?"

"According to Tom. He finally had one of the men bring it back to the ranch by the time I arrived. No reason to leave it sitting here."

"Unless Dan flew back in and needed a ride back to the ranch. He might not appreciate the long hike."

"It sat here for a week. Dan would have called by then."

"Maybe."

"You know where he is, don't you?"

He looked at her in surprise. "Of course not! Why would you say that?"

"You have a rather grim expression on your face."

He shifted in his seat and adjusted his hat. "I don't like what I see," he finally said.

"What is that?"

"We aren't more than a few hours flight time to the Mexican border. This is a hidden spot. Anyone could fly in, land, load or unload, and take off with no one being the wiser."

He looked around. "Is there another way to get here besides the way we came?"

"No. Boulders and gullies surround this flat area on three sides. The only way to reach it on land is the way we came."

"That's good to know."

Mandy thought about what Rafe said. Finally she asked, "Do you think Dan was involved in some sort of smuggling?"

"I sure as hell hope not, but at this point, we can't rule out anything. You have to admit the set-up here would be tempting to anyone moving drugs, aliens, even arms across the border."

"Dan would never do that and you know it."

"People change, Mandy. Maybe the Dan I knew wouldn't consider getting involved in the smuggling business, but his disappearance casts some real doubts in my mind."

"What if this site was being used without Dan's knowledge? Maybe he stumbled across trespassers or contraband and they caught him?"

Rafe studied Mandy's expression. "Is that what you think happened…why you think he's dead?"

"Oh, Rafe, I've come up with all kinds of ideas about what might have happened. I always come back to the same thing—if Dan was alive, we would have heard from him by now."

Rafe took her hand and said, "I hope to God you're wrong, Mandy, but I promise you this. I'm going to find out what happened to him. When I discover whoever was responsible for his disappearance, they'll answer to me."

He reached over and turned on the key, starting the engine. "I'd like to have some idea of how widely known this place happens to be."

"Tom may be able to give you information on that. Or James."

He turned the Jeep around and headed toward the house. "Then I'll talk to both of them. First thing in the morning I'm going to be out here exploring those arroyos. All sorts of things could be hidden in there. In fact, I may plan to camp out here for a few days and see what I can find out."

"I'll come with you."

He smiled. "No, you won't. I can move around by myself and no one will know I'm out here. Two people, unless they're both highly trained, would give my presence away."

"I want to do something to help."

"Then help keep Tom and his men away from the area. I don't want some innocent bystander stumbling around down here. It wouldn't hurt to run a background check on the help, as well. It's possible that one or more of them aren't all that innocent."

"You think he was kidnapped?"

"It's a possibility."

"Wouldn't someone be asking for ransom?"

"Not if they're holding him to ensure his silence."

"Then wouldn't they just kill him and be done with it?"

When he didn't answer, she realized that she'd once again voiced her biggest fear. Rafe's silence indicated to her that he couldn't argue with her logic.

Rafe pulled the Jeep into the driveway. "Do me a favor," he said once they entered the house.

"What's that?"

"See if you can contact James Williams for me."

She glanced at her watch. "He should be at his office."

"Make certain. If he is, we'll go in to see him now."

She was put through immediately.

"How's my favorite female?" James said, when he answered.

Mandy made a face. "Hello, James. I was wondering if I could come into town to talk to you this afternoon, if you have time."

"Honey, I've always got time for you. You know that. How about dinner? I could have it catered at my place. Of course, if that makes you uncomfortable we could—"

"Uh, James. I have someone with me I want you to meet."

There was a pause. "Someone? As in a male someone? As in a special male?" Each question was delivered in a frostier voice.

She glanced at Rafe who couldn't hear James. Maybe this would be a very good way to discourage James without committing herself. "Rafe and I go back a long ways," she finally replied, allowing James to read whatever he wished into her statement. She watched as Rafe rubbed his knuckle across his lips, hiding a smile. He might find it amusing, but she disliked James's manner toward her.

"Maybe you'd better meet me here at the office."

"Fine. We'll be there within the hour." She hung up and waited for Rafe to comment on the conversation.

Instead he said, "Let's go before the traffic gets too bad."

They drove to Austin without speaking. Mandy realized that she was getting used to Rafe and his long silences. The boy she remembered had always been quiet, but back then she'd talked enough for three people. Now, she discovered she had very little to say to the man. If she was honest with herself, she was a little intimidated by his quiet air of competence. He was definitely a person who she would want to have on her side and not working against her.

Mandy directed him to the plant that Dan and James had started several years ago. As they turned into a circular driveway, Rafe saw a wooden sign framed by limestone. Deeply etched into the wood was the name of the company—DSC Corporation. The new building looked like what it was—a warehouse with offices in front. The landscaping had been chosen to withstand the hot Texas summers.

The parking lot for employees was filled with late-model automobiles. In short, the business gave off an aura of efficiency and success.

"What arrangements has Dan made for the business, in case something happens to one of the partners?"

She glanced at him in surprise. "I have no idea."

Rafe got out of the truck and came around to help her out. She was surprised at his courtesy, then ashamed of her reaction. Rafe had always been courteous to her and to her mother. It was just that his politeness toward them didn't fit his overall image.

Rafe could feel Mandy's nervousness. He couldn't figure out if she was uneasy around him or uncomfortable with the upcoming meeting. He saw no reason to question her. He wasn't certain that she was conscious of her behavior at the moment.

He offered her his hand to step down out of the truck. She took it willingly enough, but as soon as her feet were on the ground, she quickly stepped away from him.

He almost smiled. Her instincts were good; he'd give her that. If she had any idea how much he wanted to scoop her up in his arms and carry her off for a few days of intense lovemaking, she would be even more skittish than she was now.

How could he fault James Williams's reaction to her when his was just as strong? He deliberately placed his hand at the small of her back and guided her to the front door of Dan's business.

As soon as they stepped inside the refreshingly cool office, the receptionist smiled and said, "Good afternoon, Ms. Crenshaw. Mr. Williams is expecting you." She eyed Rafe uncertainly. He smiled at her as reassuringly as possible and wondered why her face flushed in response. She smiled in return and ducked her head.

Rafe waited while Mandy tapped on the door. He heard

a strong, masculine voice respond and Mandy opened the door and walked into the office. Rafe followed.

James Williams looked to be thirty or so, the same age as Rafe and Dan. Of medium height, he possessed a slender build and wore a suit obviously tailored to fit. Success radiated from the man.

"James, this is Rafe McClain. He, Dan and I grew up together." She turned to Rafe. "James Williams, Dan's partner."

James stood and walked around the desk. "I'm pleased to meet you, Rafe. Any friend of the Crenshaws is automatically a friend of mine." James had a narrow face, with a silver gaze that seemed to take in and process data with lightning speed. Rafe shook his hand, noticing the firm grip without responding to it.

Rafe acknowledged the greeting with a nod, allowing Mandy to control their side of the conversation. He watched James as he returned his attention to the woman. His smile became more intimate. James took Mandy's hand and said, "It's good to see you, Mandy."

She cleared her throat. "Rafe wants to talk to you about Dan's disappearance, James."

The smile faded. "I wish you wouldn't worry so, Mandy. Dan has taken these long trips out of town before. I've explained all of that."

Rafe spoke from behind them. "Then explain it to me, if you will."

James tensed at his tone. With a show of reluctance, James stepped back from Mandy and said, "Why don't we all sit down if we're going to visit a while."

Visit, huh? Interesting take on their sudden appearance, Rafe decided. More polite than to call it an interrogation, perhaps. Rafe knew quite well that James didn't consider their showing up at his office a friendly get together.

The office wasn't large. Besides the desk and chair there

were only two other padded chairs in the room. It wasn't difficult to decide who sat where.

Once ensconced behind the desk, James folded his hands and confided to Rafe with a man-to-man condescension that set Rafe's teeth on edge, "I've been doing my best to reassure Mandy that there is no reason in the world for her to be concerned about Dan. I'm sure that he will—"

"When's the last time you spoke with him?" Rafe asked bluntly.

James's head jerked as though he'd been physically struck. He cleared his throat before glancing down at his desk calendar. "I'm not really certain."

"Today, yesterday, last week, last month?"

James frowned. "Obviously it has been a week or more." He looked at Mandy. "When did you come down here?"

"I arrived ten days ago, three days after Dan turned up missing."

James shook his head in obvious concern. "I really do wish you'd stop referring to Dan as missing, Mandy. Just because we don't know where he is at the moment doesn't mean anything is wrong."

"Mandy tells me that you generally hear from Dan when he's traveling. Now you're saying you haven't heard from him. I have to agree with Mandy's take on this situation. From what I can gather, no one has heard from him. I consider that serious enough to start looking for answers."

Mandy looked at Rafe. "Not to mention that you received—" Rafe gave a quick shake to his head causing Mandy to stop speaking.

James didn't miss the byplay. "You received something?" he asked. "From Dan?"

Rafe smiled. "Nothing recent, I assure you. Dan and I aren't the best of correspondents." He continued to lounge in his chair without taking his eyes off the other man. "Do you have a calendar of his appointments?" Rafe asked.

"I'm afraid not. He kept his calendar with him since he moved around so much. He made his own appointments. He really wasn't here in the office all that often. We communicated mostly by phone."

"So you have no idea who he might be seeing if, as you say, he's on an extended business trip."

"That's right. We each have our own area of the business for which we're responsible, which seldom overlaps. It's a good working relationship."

"Had he leased a plane?"

"No. I would have had to okay an expense of that nature." He smiled. "It's a checks-and-balances sort of thing, you understand."

"Then how do you suppose he left the ranch, if not by plane?"

"Oh, he probably did leave by plane, just not one that we leased. One of our clients probably picked him up there. It wouldn't be the first time."

"Do you ever have supplies shipped for the factory via the ranch?"

James paused just a little too long in Rafe's estimation before answering. "Sometimes. Not often."

"Does anyone else use the airstrip?"

"Not that I'm aware. Of course, I have no way of knowing."

Rafe continued to watch James. The man was one cool customer. He could see what Mandy was talking about. He was being a little patronizing, which always put Rafe's teeth on edge. "I think that's all my questions for now," Rafe finally said. "If I have any more, I'll give you a call."

James eyebrows went up. "Then you're going to investigate this so-called disappearance?"

"Yes, I am." He chose not to reveal anything more. He didn't like this man's attitude. It was too cavalier, considering he hadn't seen or spoken to his business partner in some time, had no idea where he might be and showed little interest in finding out. He also conveyed annoyance that someone else was going to investigate. On a hunch, he said, "Would you show us Dan's office? I assume he has one."

James shoved his chair back and stood, a picture of impatience and irritation. "I suppose. But whatever it is you expect to find there, I'm afraid you're going to be disappointed. As I said, he was seldom in the office."

He walked over to another door, not the one they had entered, and opened it. Waving his hand with a flourish, he said, "There you are. Look all you want." He glanced at his watch. "If you'll excuse me, I need to get back to work."

Rafe stepped back and allowed Mandy to walk into the room before he followed and closed the connecting door. The office had an unused air about it, which wasn't surprising. It was clean and uncluttered, with the usual desk items neatly aligned in front of the large, comfortable-looking chair. Rafe went over and sat down. It was every bit as comfortable as it appeared. He leaned back and put his hands behind his head. "Nice. Dan certainly believes in his comforts."

Mandy sat down in one of the visitor chairs. "Yes." She smiled. "He was so proud of setting up his own office and being in business for himself."

A quick glance around the walls revealed Dan's academic credentials. He'd graduated from Harvard with honors and picked up a master's degree in business, as well. Good for him.

Rafe checked the drawers and was surprised to see they weren't locked. He found some files with lists of businesses, no doubt customers or potential customers.

There was no calendar of appointments, no diary of events, nothing that would give him a clue to Dan's whereabouts. Everything he found was typical…except for the newspaper jammed in the back of the file drawer. He pulled it out. It was the Austin daily paper, the first two sections, which included national and local news. Rafe glanced at the date. June 29, two days before the date Dan had spoken to Tom.

He stood and held out his hand to Mandy. "Let's go." He took the paper with him. Dan might have stored it away because he hadn't finished reading it. However, there was a slight chance that there was something he might have wanted to save. Rafe would go over it once they returned to the ranch.

Rafe walked around the desk, took Mandy's hand, and they returned to the reception area. He nodded to the eagerly smiling receptionist, who fervently wished them a nice evening. Rafe made a mental note to return to Dan's office to speak to some of the employees when James wasn't there. He had a hunch they might be more cooperative than James had been.

"Not much there," Mandy said, once they left the building.

"I'm not so sure," Rafe replied. "Sometimes you learn more from someone by what he's not saying." They walked to the truck. Rafe unlocked it and helped Mandy inside. Once he joined her and turned on the engine to get the air conditioner to cool the hot cab. "Personally, I think he's lying."

"About what?"

"I'd be willing to bet a bundle he either knows where Dan is, or knows why Dan disappeared. In fact, I have a strong hunch he's actually behind Dan's disappearance."

Six

Heavy traffic surrounded them once they returned to the thoroughfare that led out of town. After waiting in a long line through two signal light sequences without reaching the intersection, Rafe said, "Let's grab a bite to eat and wait for the traffic to thin out. I can't believe this congestion."

Mandy glanced around, only now becoming aware of her surroundings. Her mind had been replaying Rafe's remarks, wondering if James was trying to hide something. "Austin's been growing while you were away. Unfortunately the highways haven't kept up."

He pulled into a restaurant on South Lamar Street and waited until they were inside, seated, and had given their orders before he said, "I'm beginning to get a bad feeling about this. It isn't natural that James isn't worried about Dan, unless he knows where he is. There's no reason to keep his whereabouts a secret unless they're involved in something illegal. If so, I wish I knew what."

"You mean because of the airstrip?"

"And James's attitude."

"Then do you think the ranch is being used for some kind of smuggling?"

"The little I've learned is pointing in that direction."

"What do you think is being smuggled? Aliens? Drugs?"

He rubbed his forehead and sighed. "It might make it easier if I had a clue."

Now that she was facing him, Mandy studied Rafe, adjusting to the man he had become. He looked tired. Was it any wonder? He'd flown in from Eastern Europe late last night. Even with several hours' sleep, his body must still be complaining, but he hadn't stopped all day. She watched him pick up his glass of water and drink. She had a sudden urge to stroke his jaw and attempt to ease his weariness. All her lectures to herself dissipated when she was in his presence.

There had always been something about him that drew her. She would be lying to herself if she pretended that magnetic force wasn't still working.

"It's tough, coming back after all these years, isn't it?" she asked.

He set the glass down with a careful movement. She knew Rafe never liked talking about himself. He may have changed over the years since she'd last seen him, but the boy she remembered was very much present in the man across from her.

"Yeah," he finally said, admitting what they both knew.

Mandy wanted so much to break through the shell in which he encased himself. Even Dan, admittedly his best and perhaps only friend, had never been able to draw Rafe out. Well, she was going to give it her best shot. For some reason she couldn't quite explain even to herself, Mandy sensed that Rafe was feeling his isolation today in ways he'd never faced before.

"I have a hunch it was no accident that you stayed away from this part of the country," she said, offering him an opening to discuss his feelings.

The waiter arrived with their iced tea and salads. When he left, Rafe picked up his iced tea. He paused with the glass halfway to his mouth and said, "I had no intention of ever coming back to Texas when I left here."

There it was, what had been between them—unspoken— since he had arrived.

Mandy leaned toward him. With an intensity that made her voice quiver slightly, she said, "If I could redo what I did that night, Rafe, I would. Please believe that, if nothing else. What happened was all my fault. I've lived with that guilt. I was so ashamed of the way my father behaved, the way he automatically blamed you, the way he treated you."

He shrugged. "Don't be." He picked up his fork and began to rearrange his salad. "If I had been in his shoes, I would have done the same thing. You were an innocent young girl and you had no business being with me that night."

"But it wasn't your fault I was."

"You think not? You think I didn't know what I was doing when I danced with you, encouraged you? I wanted you that night, Mandy, don't ever doubt it. I knew how I felt was wrong, but when you showed up at my door, I didn't turn you away. I didn't stop the kiss. If your father hadn't shown up when he did, I can't say, even now, that I would have stopped in time. Your father could see how close to being out of control I was. He was right. That was a lousy way to repay his hospitality and he had every right to kick my ass off the property. I deserved it."

She couldn't believe what she was hearing...what he was admitting. Her body responded to his words as though he'd caressed her. "I always thought it was me," she whispered, her heart racing, "imagining things that night about how you felt."

He shook his head, frowning at her words. "It wasn't your imagination. I'd been aware of you for a long time. I kept telling myself to ignore you, that you were just a kid. I made myself adopt Dan's attitude toward you and treated you like a sister. But I couldn't carry it off that night. You looked so grown up and you felt so good in my arms. I lost my head."

"Thank you for telling me this, Rafe. That scene has haunted me for years."

"Be glad your dad came looking for you when he did. He did the right thing."

She propped her chin on her hand. "I tried to explain to him the next morning what really had happened, you know, but by then you'd already left. I guess my mother was the one who thought I might have gotten carried away that night, watching us dance, and sent him to look for me. I heard her talking to my dad the next day, after he'd calmed down. She was taking up for you, talking about hormones and youth and reminding him of when he was that age." She smiled. "That's probably why he reacted so strongly. He'd been that age once, himself."

They ate their salads in silence before Rafe said, "I got over all of that a long time ago, Mandy. Things worked out the way they needed to for both of us. You hung on to your innocence a while longer and I didn't have to live with the burden of being the man who took it from you. I got on with my life."

"But you didn't go on to college, did you?"

He suddenly became engrossed in setting his empty plate aside and she thought he wasn't going to answer her. He took a breadstick from the basket and broke it in two before he said, "No, I didn't go to college. Under the circumstances, I thought it better to leave the area."

"So I knocked you out of your education, as well," she said with self-disgust.

He shook his head. "Don't take all the credit. Remember that I was going to try it. I might have dropped out after the first semester, anyway. I was rarin' to see the world back then. Too impatient to wait."

"Did you hop an ocean freighter?"

He looked at her in surprise. "You still remember that?"

He really didn't have a clue. For some reason she felt it was important that he know the truth about her feelings. It was the very least that she owed him, as far as she was concerned. "I have never forgotten anything about that night, Rafe. There were times when I fell asleep remembering each dance, the song that was playing, what we said, the way you looked, the way I felt. I would lie there wondering where you were, what you were doing, and if you ever thought about me."

He swallowed, then looked around as though hoping their food would arrive to distract her and the present topic of conversation.

"Where did you go after you left the ranch?" she asked when it was obvious he wasn't going to respond to her admittedly provocative statement.

"I walked to Austin. I tried to catch a ride at first, but no one was going to stop and pick up a hitchhiker at that time of night."

"Oh, Rafe. That was much too far to walk."

"I didn't have anything better to do at the time. It took a couple of days. I found a barn to sleep in. I could have gotten a ride the next day, but I needed the time to rethink my plans."

"What did you end up doing?"

"I joined the Army. I needed the security afforded me in the service. I ended up writing Dan when I was in basic training and he answered. He left for college right after that, so we kept in touch."

"Did you like the Army?"

"Like it?" He considered. "It made a man of me. I went into Special Forces. You grow up quick. Actually I managed to get several college credits while I was in the military. I did all right."

"And you were good at what you did."

He gave her a level look. "Yes."

Their orders appeared and Rafe looked relieved. They ate with little conversation. Over coffee and dessert, he asked, "So what do you do in Dallas?"

"I work with Children's Services. I'm a licensed psychologist and I do evaluations on children and their living conditions. Suggest changes in their environment if I feel a child would be better served. It's no longer automatically assumed that a child is better off with his or her parents."

Rafe thought back over his childhood. He wondered if his mother and two sisters were still alive, or whether his father had succeeded in destroying them as he'd tried so hard to destroy him. Rafe had made no effort to contact any of them once he was safely away. He wondered if any of his family still lived in the East Texas area he had left at fourteen. Maybe he'd check into it while he was in the state, just for the hell of it.

"What are you thinking?" she asked.

"Nothing worth repeating." He reached for his wallet and picked up the ticket. "Ready to go?"

Once back in the truck, they followed highway 290 west out of town.

"Are you still with the Army?" Mandy asked after a few miles.

"No."

"You said last night you were a consultant."

"Uh-huh."

"What kind?"

"I teach people how to stay alive in less than hospitable surroundings."

"You learned that in the military?"

"Oh, yeah."

"You like what you do?"

"Well enough. As you suggested, I'm good at what I do."

"Have you ever thought about moving back to the States?"

He glanced at her and smiled. "There's no real demand for my kind of work in the States, Miss Mandy."

"Which means no."

"Pretty much. Yeah."

She sighed. Well, at least she knew Rafe's intentions. He would do what he could to find out what had happened to Dan and then he would disappear once again. That shouldn't surprise her.

The sun was setting when they pulled up in front of the ranch house. Mandy got out of the truck and waited while Rafe parked in the long storage shed near the barn. She watched him as he stepped down from the truck, pocketed the keys and then leisurely walked toward her.

She could feel her heart thumping in her chest, her pulse singing and a tingle of anticipation and expectancy flood her system. Once he joined her at the gate to the inner yard, they strolled up the walkway together.

Ranger came tearing around the corner to greet them, his tail wildly lashing. Rafe knelt and loved on him, murmuring something to him that Ranger seemed to enjoy. Mandy had a hunch Tom may have lost Ranger's loyalty for the length of Rafe's stay.

Once inside, Rafe said, "I think I'll go take a shower. Maybe I'll be able to cool off. Guess I haven't adjusted to the humidity as yet."

Mandy nodded, unable to say a word. Her feelings for this man were tumbling out from wherever she had stored them years ago. She felt inundated with emotion. Rafe was back, was all she could think. He was back temporarily, but he was here now. The question was, what did she intend to do about it?

Mandy wandered restlessly through the house, trying to deal with her tumultuous feelings. Having Rafe back in her life, even temporarily, was a turning point for her. Being able to talk about what had happened twelve years ago had given her the opportunity to release all those pent-up emotions that had kept her so locked up inside.

The question was, what could she do about it?

Mandy walked outside and sat down on the front steps. Ranger trotted up and stretched out beside her.

She had been in such turmoil these past few days that she needed some time to think about what was happening. Her safe little world had dissolved so that nothing seemed real anymore.

Dan was gone. That thought was always there, lurking. What was she going to do without Dan in her life? She didn't care if he'd done something wrong, if he was in trouble. What she wanted to know was that he was alive. Everything after that could be dealt with.

Now Rafe had suddenly appeared in her life again and their talk today had cleared away so much of the baggage that she had carried for years. She felt lighter, freer, more willing to let go of all her old perceptions.

Outside of Dan, Rafe was the most important person in her life. She knew he was scarred in many ways because of his childhood. She had worked with many children from similar backgrounds, children who had shut off their emotions rather than take a chance on being hurt again.

She probably understood Rafe better now than he understood himself. She could keep her distance and allow him to do whatever he could do to locate Dan. Sooner or later he would leave.

Unless…

What if she could show him another way to deal with his feelings rather than to keep them locked away? What if she could show him how deeply she felt for him, how strong her love and support could be? Would it make a difference to him? Would he be willing to open himself up to a relationship with her?

She shivered at the thought. He had admitted to feelings that he'd had twelve years ago. That was a start. Loving Rafe would be the biggest risk she'd ever taken in her life. He was no longer a vulnerable child, but a man who'd grown tougher as he'd gotten older, who knew no other life than one of being alone.

Did she have the nerve to confront him with her own feelings, to take the chance of making her hopes and dreams a reality? Because if she didn't, she knew that he would continue to keep his distance and disappear from her life once more.

She'd been given a second chance with this man. At a time when she was grieving for the possible loss of her brother, she was also faced with the almost certain loss of the man who had haunted her for years.

What did she have to lose—besides her dignity, pride and self-esteem? Was it worth the risk in hopes of gaining so much more if she could finally open Rafe up to the possibility of sharing her life, of forming a bond with her that might eventually become the basis of a family?

She could play it safe, of course, and keep her feelings to herself. She could play it safe and live with the knowledge for the rest of her life that she'd been too afraid of being embarrassed and possibly humiliated to find out if the boy she fell for all those years ago still existed within the hard shell of the man he was today.

Whatever she decided, she knew she had very little time and absolutely no idea how to go about implementing such a plan. She stroked Ranger's head and watched the sun set while she considered her options.

Rafe stood under the cool spray of water, willing his body to relax and calm down. The last thing he'd needed to hear today was that Mandy had spent any of her time during the past several years thinking of him. The thought scared the hell out of him, even if he wasn't certain why it should. There was nothing between them now. There was no reason to think anything would change during the time he was here.

At least she appeared to be more relaxed with him as the day wore on. In fact, she'd gotten downright chatty at the restaurant. She'd reminded him of the Mandy he used to know. He just wished she had chosen to discuss anything other than the last night he'd spent on the ranch.

Sure he'd been incensed by her father's attitude toward him, treating him like some kind of white trash, throwing it up to him that he wouldn't have had a place to live without his charity.

Rafe had been so angry that he'd been glad to throw everything he owned into a backpack and leave the ranch. He hadn't wanted to stick around if that was the way the old man had felt about him.

But it had hurt because Rafe had always respected the elder Crenshaw, thought him a fair man and looked up to him. Rafe had known that Mandy's father never would have struck him, regardless of how angry he was. Mr. Crenshaw had been the first man he'd ever trusted. It had shattered him to realize that the man may have been right about him. He might have seduced Amanda if her father hadn't shown up. What kind of scum did that make him?

He'd known that there was no way that he could face any of them after that. So he had left, determined never to look back. He set out to prove to himself, at least, that he wasn't a worthless piece of trash and that he could amount to something.

Writing to Dan had been against all his strongly held beliefs that he needed to forget the Crenshaws. The thing was, basic training had been hard, even tougher than he had imagined. Plus, he'd been homesick, which was a laugh. He hadn't had a home to miss, but it didn't seem to matter.

He'd addressed the letter to Dan because he was sure that Mandy wouldn't want anything more to do with him and he suspected her mom was just as angry as her dad. But Dan had always been there for him.

He still remembered the day Dan's letter arrived. It was the first time his name had been mentioned at mail call. He'd stared at the envelope with the cramped handwriting that was typically Dan and fought the tears.

Dan had remembered him. He'd written him.

Rafe carried the letter with him all that day. He waited until just before lights out to open it. Again, in typical Dan fashion, the letter was short and to the point. He chewed Rafe out for leaving, no matter what his dad might have said to him in anger. He reminded him that he'd just blown his education by taking off in a huff, and that he sure must like the idea of a uniform to have gone into the Army so fast.

He'd also told him to stay in touch and that as soon as Dan got to Harvard, he'd send Rafe his address.

There were times in the twelve years since then when Rafe had been ready to give up, times when the life he had chosen had seemed so godforsaken that he could think of no good reason why he should hang on. Then the memory of Dan would pop into his head and he could practically hear Dan yelling at him, poking at him, forcing him to keep going.

"I hope you can hear me, Dan, wherever you are," he

muttered. "Whatever hole you've dug for yourself, don't give up, okay? Hang in there. I'm going to find you—some way, somehow."

Rafe dried off and tied the towel around his waist. He was too tired to do any more investigating today. Maybe he'd read that paper he'd brought from Dan's office. See if he could figure out why Dan saved it. He'd tossed it on the kitchen table when they'd gotten back from town. He would pull on his jeans and go get it.

He opened the bathroom door and stepped into Dan's bedroom…then stopped in his tracks. Mandy sat on the side of the bed, obviously waiting for him.

"Mandy?" he managed to say, sounding strangled. "What are you doing in here?"

Her flushed face seemed to grow even pinker with his question. She stood and he noticed that she had a death grip on the bedpost. She started to speak, swallowed, then tried again.

"Rafe, I—um—I'm no longer fifteen," she managed to say before running out of breath.

Her nervousness calmed him down, but her presence in his room totally destroyed the effort he'd made in the shower to convince his body she was off limits. He grabbed his towel as it threatened to slide off his rapidly changing body.

"I am very much aware of that," he said grimly, gripping his towel.

"I guess I've still not learned not to come to your room and throw myself at you."

"Is that what you're doing?" He sounded hoarse.

She nodded. "I want to make love with you. I want to erase what happened before and replace it with new memories. Is that asking too much of you?" Her voice faltered at the end so that he barely heard her.

Dear God, this was like one of the medicated, fevered

fantasy dreams he'd had while recuperating from one of his numerous wounds—Mandy, offering herself to him. In his dreams, he'd never questioned the opportunity presented. He'd eagerly accepted her offer.

"I don't think that's a very good idea, Mandy. I—"

He wasn't certain what he'd intended to say. The thought was wiped out of his mind when she let go of the bedpost and removed first her blouse, then her bra, her cheeks glowing with color.

He moved toward her as though magnetized by her presence. Her gaze locked with his and she stood there, waiting to see what he would do.

Never had he fought so hard to resist anything in his life. Hadn't he managed to prove to himself over the years that he had an infinite supply of self-control? But nothing had tempted him the way Mandy could. And like the boy he'd been, he still couldn't keep his hands off her.

He lifted his hand and brushed it against her cheek. "Aw, Mandy, you're so sweet." He saw that her gaze had dropped to the towel that could no longer disguise his reaction to her. She smiled and stepped closer, pressing her bare breasts against his chest and kissing him with an eager innocence that belied her twenty-seven years.

She'd certainly been right. She was no longer fifteen years old. Her kiss had steam coming out of his ears. He wrapped his arms around her, allowing the towel to fall to the floor.

Mandy sighed, her breath whispering over his lips. She placed her hands on his chest and lovingly smoothed them across the surface, allowing gravity to take over until her hands rested on his erection. She stroked him, her fingers barely touching the surface.

Rafe no longer remembered why it wasn't a good idea for him to make love to Mandy. All he knew was that if he didn't hang on to some semblance of control, he was going to explode right now.

He forced himself to step away from her, but he couldn't resist cupping his hands beneath her beautiful breasts and caressing them. Her whimper almost destroyed him.

He reached for her jeans with shaking hands and unfastened them, shoving them down her legs before he lifted her and placed her on the bed. She watched him, her eyes glistening as he pulled them the rest of the way off before he stretched out beside her.

"It's been too long for me," he said gruffly. "I can't hang on much longer."

She reached for him and pulled him over her. "It doesn't matter, Rafe. Just love me."

"This is what I used to dream about," he murmured, running his hand along a line from her throat to the top of her thighs. "You, lying in my bed, wearing nothing but your beautiful smile." He shifted so that he was touching her and paused only long enough to be sure she was ready for him before he claimed her. He was thankful she was ready because he couldn't wait.

In an embarrassingly short time, he collapsed against her, almost sobbing in an effort to get air in his lungs. She clung to him, stroking his back and whispering soothing words to him.

With a groan he pulled himself away from her and stretched out on the bed beside her, his eyes closed, his humiliation complete.

Well, so much for that, he thought irritably. *I might as well be a teenage boy for all the finesse I showed. Hell, I wasn't able to give her any pleasure at all.*

"I'm sorry," he finally managed to say when he was able to talk.

"Don't be," she replied. He opened his eyes. She was propped up on her elbow looking down at him. "We have all night, you know. There's nobody around to interrupt us," she added, with a shy but mischievous smile.

"Aw, Mandy, what am I going to do with you?" he whispered, his chest aching with more feeling than he could possibly express.

"Love me?" she suggested.

He didn't know about love. It wasn't part of his world. But he could be gentle with her. He could help her find some of the pleasure that his uncontrolled efforts just now had deprived her of. She didn't appear to be upset, not if that smile was any indication. He shifted so that he was facing her and felt himself beginning to relax.

"Let me look at you," she said, leaning over him. "Let me feed all my girlish imaginings with real data." She ran her palms along his jaw, leaning down to kiss him before beginning her voyage of discovery.

During her exploration, she somehow found each and every nick in his hide and demanded to know what had caused them. He answered her by wrapping his arms around her and rolling her beneath him. Her touch had aroused him so quickly he was astounded. He couldn't seem to get enough of her.

She curled around him, her arms and legs holding him firmly against her. He traced kisses across her throat and down to her breasts, then caressed the tips with his tongue, toying with them until they became hard nubs of sensitive flesh.

By the time he joined them again, she was quivering, her breathing ragged. He moved slowly, watching her, waiting. He needed her to enjoy this. He continued exploring her body with his mouth, keeping his rhythm slow and easy. He leaned closer and kissed her, his tongue delving into her mouth with the same rhythm as his hips. His movement picked up in intensity and yet, she seemed to be resisting what she was feeling.

"Let go, Mandy, just…let go for me," he whispered. His control was gone. Again. Damn. With a sense of frustration he allowed his body to take over, moving faster, harder, mindlessly striving for completion.

Then he felt her convulse from deep inside and he breathed his thanks. Her inner muscles contracted and she let out a high moan, clutching his shoulders with a steel grip. He was right there with her each and every step of the way, making one final lunge that drew everything out of him—his heart, his spirit, his very life force—and passed them to her.

Rafe managed to hang onto enough awareness to roll to her side before he let go and sank into the bed's welcoming softness. He gathered her into his arms and held her close as he drifted into peaceful oblivion.

He was aroused sometime later by movement. He fought off the fog of near unconsciousness long enough to remember where he was. "What is it?" he mumbled.

"I'm cold," she whispered. "I was trying to get some of the covers out from under us."

They had fallen asleep without pulling the sheet and spread down. He rolled and lifted off the bed. As soon as he moved the covers, he stretched back on the bed.

"Come here," he murmured, holding out his arm where she'd been sleeping.

"You'll probably sleep better if I go back to my bed."

"Don't you dare," he replied gruffly.

She slipped under the covers and plastered herself along his side.

"Still cold?" he asked.

"Not now."

"Me, either." He was also awake enough to know that he wasn't going to waste having Mandy in bed with him by sleeping through it.

Whether it was the late hour when the night is hushed and time seems to stand still, or whether the first rush of sexual need finally had been met, this time Rafe took his time loving Mandy. He lazily explored every inch of her body, kissing and caressing her until she was sobbing with the need for completion. She stirred restlessly, her legs shifting whenever he touched her. She lifted her hips to him in a silent plea.

When he finally entered her, he moved swiftly. He'd teased them both almost past bearing. Now they rode together for the finish, both crying out when they reached that particular peak, holding on to each other as though fearful of being torn apart.

They lay there in the darkness, still entwined, while they slowly regained their breath. Rafe had no idea of the time, but he didn't care. He hadn't planned to return to the airstrip until daylight. He had time to lie there and savor the experience of having Mandy in his arms.

"Rafe?"

"Hmm."

"Tell me something."

He released a contented sigh. "What do you want me to tell you?"

"About your parents."

He lay there staring into the blackness. "My parents? What about them?"

"I want to know about you. You never talked about them in all the years you lived here. Would you tell me about them now?"

"What do you want to know?"

"Mmm...names? Where they're from? How they met? Those kinds of things."

He was too relaxed to get uptight thinking about his parents. Nothing could touch the cocoon of contentment he was presently enjoying.

"My father's name is Luke McClain. My mother is Maria Teresa Salinas. My dad was in the military and stationed in South Texas when they first met. Mom was seventeen."

When he didn't say anything else, she prompted him.
"They met, they fell in love, they got married. Right?"

"I don't know about the falling in love part. Mom got
pregnant. Her father was ready to kill somebody from what
I understand, so my father married her."

"You were born then?"

"No. She gave birth to a boy. He died when he was two."

"Oh. Do you have any other brothers or sisters?"

"Two sisters."

"You are their only son."

"Yes."

"What is your full name?"

"Raphael Lucas McClain."

"Raphael. Like the angel."

"Yeah. People get confused about that all the time."

She chuckled, then nipped his shoulder with her teeth.

"Ouch!"

"What does your dad do?"

"Besides drink? He always worked in construction, but
had trouble holding a job. He was good with his
hands...when he was sober. Actually he was good with
them when he was drunk, too. I learned to stay out of his
reach about the time I learned to walk."

"When did you move to this part of the country?"

"I was eight and in the third grade. That's when I met
Dan. We were in the sixth grade when my dad took a job
in East Texas. We moved around a lot when I was growing
up, but I really enjoyed living in this area. That's why I
decided to come back here when I left East Texas."

"What did your mother say when you left?"

"I don't know. I just got tired of my dad knocking me
around. I left in the middle of the night and never went
back."

"Just like when you left here."

He was silent. "Yeah, pretty much," he finally said.

"I want you to tell me goodbye when you leave this time, Rafe. Don't leave in the middle of the night. Promise me that."

"Why? What difference does it make? I'm still leaving."

"Yes, I know. But I want to be able to tell you goodbye."

He turned to her. "I'm not leaving just yet, though," he said, nuzzling her ear and stroking her breast.

"I know," she replied, her lips searching blindly for his.

He hadn't promised her he wouldn't leave without telling her goodbye, but she had given him some things to think about...when he was in the mood to think.

Seven

The sound of steady knocking on a door somewhere finally roused Rafe. He rolled over and discovered Mandy throwing the covers back and getting out of bed, muttering something under her breath.

''Who is it?'' he mumbled.

She glanced over her shoulder, then shrugged her shoulders and headed out of the room, saying, ''Tom, probably.''

''I hope to hell you don't intend to answer the door that way!'' he growled, sitting up in bed. She had on as much clothing as he did. Zip. He heard her closet door slam and he grinned. She'd at least stopped for a robe.

He yawned, wondering what time it was. Didn't look as if the sun had been up long. He'd taken off his watch before his shower last night and had been too distracted to put it back on.

What had taken place last night wasn't at all smart on his part. As he recalled, he had made some sort of heroic effort to say no, but he'd been lying and he knew it at the time.

Now he was faced with the consequences, and he knew they would have lasting repercussions—on his peace of mind if no other way. He hadn't asked her about birth control, an oversight he'd never been guilty of before. His brain had rolled over and played dead from the moment he stepped out of the bathroom and found her in the bedroom. His body and emotions had taken over from there.

So what did he intend to do about the possibility of a pregnancy? He groaned at the thought of creating a similar situation to the one his dad had created thirty-five years ago. He wondered if we're destined as human beings to repeat the sins of our fathers down through the ages.

Rafe decided on a quick shower. If that was Tom, he needed to talk to him about his plans to go out to the airstrip and look around the area, possibly stay out a night or two. After what had happened last night, the safest thing he could do for everyone involved would be to stay away from the ranch house.

It would also be the hardest thing for him to do. He didn't have much faith in his willpower or self-control after last night.

Mandy was still tying the sash to her robe when she reached the back door and saw Tom through the glass. She threw open the door and said, "Mornin', Tom. Come on in."

She turned away and went over to start the coffee. She heard Tom enter the room behind her and close the door.

"I was worried about you, Mandy. You didn't have Ranger in the house last night. I was surprised to find him sleeping on my porch when I left my place this morning."

She continued to gather the necessary items for coffee without turning around. "I guess I should have mentioned it to you, but I figured he would be a better watch dog outside and I feel safe enough with Rafe sleeping here."

"Ah."

Mandy turned around and saw that he was standing in the middle of the large room, watching her. "Sit down, Tom, and have some coffee."

Reluctantly he moved over to the table and sat down. "Sorry about waking you up," he finally said when she made no effort to speak.

"No problem. It was time for me to be up, anyway." She was uncomfortably aware that she had on nothing beneath the thin cotton material of her robe. She set out three cups, then said, "I'll be right back. Help yourself to the coffee."

She hurried down the hall in time to hear the water cut off from Dan's bathroom. Good. There would be some water pressure. She quickly went into the hall bathroom and started the water, took a quick shower, dried and threw on her robe once again before dashing across the hall to find some clothes to put on. By the time she was dressed and headed back to the kitchen she heard the rumble of deep male voices.

Both men were seated at the table with a steaming cup in front of each of them. Rafe was telling Tom his plan to scrutinize the area around the landing strip when she walked in.

He interrupted himself and said with a smile. "Good morning, Mandy. Hope you slept well last night."

"Just fine," she muttered without looking at him. She poured herself a cup of coffee and joined the men at the table. Tom was watching them closely, looking at first one, then the other. She felt as though anyone looking at her would know that she'd spent the night making passionate love to Rafe. Not that she cared if Tom figured that out, but it was no one's business. Certainly not his.

"What are you expecting to find?" Tom finally asked Rafe when it became obvious that no one else was going to speak.

She tensed, waiting for Rafe to make a flippant comment. Instead he was quiet for a minute or two, obviously thinking. When he did respond, he sounded serious.

"I'm not really certain, but it makes sense to thoroughly check out the area where Dan was before he disappeared. Maybe I'm grasping at straws, but at the moment there's nothing else to go on. I spoke with Dan's partner yesterday." He sipped on his coffee before asking, "Do you know him?"

Tom shrugged. "I was introduced to him, once. That's about it. He doesn't come out here much."

"I find it strange, and a little suspicious that he's not concerned about Dan's continued absence."

"I had the same reaction. I waited a couple of days, and when I didn't hear from Dan, I thought maybe Mandy might have heard from him. Frankly, I don't trust his partner."

"Me, either." Rafe smiled. "At least we found something we can agree on."

Tom glanced at Mandy, then away. "I have a hunch there's several things we may agree on."

"Have you had breakfast, Tom?" Mandy asked, pushing away from the table.

He smiled. "Yeah, a couple of hours ago."

Mandy knew she was blushing. It couldn't be helped. Without saying anything to Rafe she got up and busied herself with preparing bacon, eggs and toast.

"How many hands do you have working full-time on the ranch?" Rafe asked.

"Three besides me."

"How well do you know them? Did you check references, that sort of thing?"

Tom scratched his ear. "They're all local, if that's what you mean. Guess I've known them most of my life."

"You're from around here?"

"Yeah. Grew up in Dripping Springs. Went to school there."

"Dan and I went to school in Wimberley. Is that how you met him? Through living so close to the ranch?"

"No. When he let it be known he was looking for someone to run the ranch for him, word got out and eventually I heard about it. I was raised on a ranch west of here. My family sold it when I was away at A & M. All I ever wanted to do was ranch. So taking this position worked out well for me."

"Do you know if any of the men working for you have any serious problems—drug addictions, heavy gambling, messy divorce—anything that would cause them to look for extra money?"

"Not that I know of. Why?"

Rafe shoved his hand through his hair before answering. "Hell, I don't know. It just seems to me that if someone on the ranch could set up a system of contacting others, the ranch could be used to smuggle items in and out of the country with relative ease."

Tom straightened. "Is that what you think is going on?"

"It's a theory I'm working on. What if Dan heard a plane the night he disappeared and decided to go and investigate? In doing so, he might have found out more than someone wanted him to know. So he was taken on board before he could talk about what he'd seen."

"They could have just killed him right there, if that's what they wanted to accomplish."

"But they didn't. And I think that's significant. No one wanted an investigation to be brought here to the ranch."

"Who or what is behind this?"

"There's the big question. It could be so many things that I don't want to hazard a guess." Mandy set a steaming plate of food in front of him. Rafe looked up at her and smiled. "Thanks."

His smile had the capacity to make her knees buckle. Mandy didn't trust herself to answer, so she nodded in response. She placed another plate where she'd been sitting, refilled everyone's cups, then sat down, concentrating on the food in front of her and not the man sitting so close beside her.

Tom spoke. "You think it's someone here on the ranch?"

"Not necessarily. I'm just covering all possibilities."

Tom nodded. "I'll check the men out and get back with you."

"I'd appreciate it."

"In the meantime," Tom said, rising, "I'd better get back to work." He looked down at Mandy and gave her a haunted smile. "I'll check on you later. If Rafe's going to be away, I'd feel better if you kept Ranger nearby."

Tom had never looked at her quite like that before, or if he had, she'd never noticed. Was Rafe right? Did Tom consider her more than just Dan's sister?

She liked Tom. He was a good man. Unfortunately she'd given her heart to Rafe on a summer night many years ago. Last night, she'd just made it official.

"I appreciate your concern for me, Tom," she said gently, touching his sleeve. "I'll make certain that Ranger is with me while Rafe is gone."

He nodded briskly. "Thanks. I'll see you later." He glanced at Rafe and nodded, then left, closing the door quietly behind him.

Now that they were alone, Mandy was nervous. She didn't want to start building pipe dreams just because Rafe had made love to her last night. That would be worse than foolish. After all, she was the one who had gone to him, just as she had before. Okay, so he'd admitted that he'd deliberately stirred her while dancing with her all those years ago. She couldn't accuse him of having done that yesterday. His focus had been on Dan's disappearance.

She wondered if he was going to say anything about last night.

She wondered if she should make some lighthearted comment to let him know she wasn't going to make a big deal of it.

She glanced over at him and realized that he was reading a newspaper that had been lying beside his plate. Oh, that was touching. All the time she was agonizing over how he might be feeling about last night and he'd already dismissed it and moved on to other things.

Mandy hopped up from the table and took her plate to the sink. "Are you finished with breakfast?" she asked in a carefully neutral voice.

"Mm-hmm," he absently replied.

"More coffee?"

"Uh, sure." He didn't look up from the paper.

She was tempted to pour the coffee over his head, but he might think she was upset about something...when she wasn't. Not at all.

As soon as she had the dishes taken care of, Mandy left the kitchen without saying another word. After all, what was there to say? Rafe had plainly showed her by his actions that he had no intention of allowing their lovemaking to make a difference between them.

What had she expected? When she looked back over the evening, she realized that he had opened up to her in ways he'd never done before. She'd found out about his childhood, although she hadn't been surprised by what she'd heard. What she found so disheartening was that, even as a young boy, he had the capacity of walking away and never looking back.

She hoped that just maybe she had made a dent in his armor by what they had shared last night. It hadn't just been the lovemaking, although that had been beyond belief. She'd had no idea she could feel so much pleasure with someone. He'd taught her things about herself she'd never known.

Hopefully she had done the same for him.

Perhaps he hadn't known what to say to her this morning, which is why he'd immediately become engrossed in the paper once the buffer of Tom's presence had disappeared.

The first thing she needed to do was to cultivate some patience. She was trying to undo a lifetime of self-protective training. Last night hadn't been a bad first step.

With a grin on her face, Mandy returned to Dan's bedroom and stripped the bed. She'd keep herself busy with household chores today and wait to see what happened next.

Rafe was ready to toss the paper aside, convinced there was nothing of particular notice when he spotted a small article at the bottom of page three of the first section.

"Police responded Saturday morning to a security alert from DSC Corporation. Company officials state that 1000 of their new A71-E Firestorm 900 MHz microprocessor chips had been stolen from their high security warehouse.

Company officials estimate the value of the chips to be in excess of one million dollars. Police say that in today's market, the chips are actually worth more than their weight in gold."

This article must be the reason Dan had kept the paper. Rafe considered the significance of this new information. It might have nothing to do with Dan's disappearance. But what if it did? And wasn't it odd that James made no mention of any theft problems the company had been having?

Microprocessor chips. The more he thought about it, the

more he could see a possible link-if not with Dan's disappearance, at least with the idea of smuggling.

Just think of the possibilities. There were several foreign leaders he could list, barred from doing business with the U.S., who would pay mega-bucks to get their hands on some highly-advanced technology.

James and Dan were sitting on a gold mine.

Suppose the chips hadn't been stolen at all, just reported stolen, so that they could be sold to much higher bidders?

Rafe reminded himself that Dan had contacted him, asking for his help. Dan knew very well that Rafe wouldn't go against any government sanctions. At least he hoped Dan knew him well enough to know that.

What if Dan happened to discover that the missing components and his ranch were connected to illegal activities and he needed Rafe's help to stop it? That was more like the Dan that he remembered.

He had to find Dan in order to get answers to these questions. And it was obvious he would get no help from Dan's partner.

He threw down the paper and strode through the house to the bedroom. Mandy was finishing making up the bed. He had a pang of remorse that he hadn't been able to greet her this morning the way he'd wanted to, but he knew she wouldn't have appreciated Tom witnessing his ardor.

He walked over and wrapped his arms around her from behind and kissed her on the ear. "I wanted to do this as soon as you walked into the kitchen, but I figured Tom wouldn't be amused."

She turned in his arms and draped her arms around his shoulders. "That's very thoughtful of you," she replied, returning his kiss.

Rafe had to keep his mind on what he was supposed to be doing. Reluctantly he stepped away from her. "I've got to go, Mandy. I'm going to spend most of the day at the airstrip, looking around those canyons. I'm not sure when I'll be back.''

She smiled. ''Wait a minute. Let me put some sandwiches together for you,'' she said, and hurried out of the room.

He slowly followed her down the hallway. Damn, but he was in big trouble. He had to concentrate on Dan for now and he was having a tough time distancing himself from all the emotions that had been stirred in him last night. He still couldn't believe Mandy's loving and generous gift.

He'd always told himself that nothing could be as good as his fantasies about her, but they faded into insignificance compared to actually making love to her. He knew he was in danger of losing his perspective on things. It was a good thing he was going to be gone today. It would give him time to regain his equilibrium.

After placing the lunch package in his backpack, Rafe gave Mandy a wave and quickly stepped outside. The ranch yard appeared to be deserted.

He struck out down the road that eventually led to the landing strip.

''Need a ride?'' Tom called.

Rafe paused and looked around. Tom stood in the doorway of the barn.

''No, thanks. I need the exercise.''

Tom was the kind of man that Mandy needed. It was obvious to Rafe that Tom was more than a little interested in Mandy, regardless of her protests to the contrary. Maybe the man hadn't spoken up, yet.

Rafe didn't want to get in his way. He knew that he would be no good to her. Mandy deserved so much more than he was capable of giving. He needed to remember that and not take advantage of her nurturing nature.

Whatever had possessed him to talk about his family after

all this time? They were part of his history, a part that didn't touch on the present time at all.

If you drop your guard you'll get hit in a vulnerable spot, he reminded himself. The problem was he hadn't been aware he had any vulnerable spots until Mandy showed up in his life again.

Who was he kidding? He was just as vulnerable where Dan was concerned.

"Come on, Dan," he muttered. "Give me some clues. Help me figure out what the hell is going on."

Out of habit he soon left the road and made his way through the cover of trees and foliage. If anyone was out there, he didn't want them to know he was, too. Not that he expected to spot anyone, but he was used to taking no chances.

By the time he reached the landing strip Rafe was focused on the job at hand. He circled the area until he got into the breaks in the land, a tumbled mass of granite, rock and shale. He jumped into one of the gullies and followed it, looking for anything that hadn't been placed there by Mother Nature.

He stopped about midafternoon to eat the lunch Mandy had prepared for him, drank water from a thermos and looked at the inhospitable terrain—rugged hills, faults in the land, granite outcrops. From where he sat, it looked as though there was an indentation in the rock face about half-way up the wall of this particular dry wash.

He decided to investigate.

He'd walked past the place earlier but had missed it. The angle of the sun and ensuing shadows caused a brief illumination of the area, highlighting what looked to be a deep recess in the wall. Rafe's heart picked up. He wasn't sure what he thought he'd found, but his increased heart rate told him he was hoping for something.

There was no way to the place from down here. It took him a while to circle out of the gully and locate the same place from above.

Because he was watching so closely, he spotted a thin trail leading down over the side. An animal could be using it for a lair. It could also house a nice nest of rattlesnakes.

Once he was on a level with it, Rafe could see a cave that seemed large enough for a man to stand upright. It could be filled with bats, since the Hill Country abounded in bat caves, but he doubted it. By now, he would have gotten a whiff of the distinctive—and exceedingly unappetizing—scent to indicate their presence.

There was a small ledge in front of the cave that hadn't been visible from either above or below. Moving with deliberate stealth he edged closer until he could see inside.

He let out a breath and stepped into the cave. The roof rapidly lowered toward the back, but the livable space was about eight-foot square. Livable was the operative word. There were supplies here. Human supplies. A few canned goods, traces of a fire, a couple of small pots and a battered bedroll occupied the area.

Could this be where Dan was hiding?

Rafe couldn't buy that. It wasn't his style. No, this was someone's living quarters. But why?

There was only one way to find out. He would have to find an observation point and watch to see who returned to the place.

Within minutes he was back on level ground, looking around for a likely place to set up a stakeout.

He spotted a cluster of live oaks approximately fifty yards away. The trees were probably a hundred years old or older, thick enough that he could climb high enough to be comfortable and set up a temporary aerie while he waited.

After reconnoitering, he chose a likely looking place high

up in one of the middle trees. He would be effectively camouflaged but would have a clear view of the area where a person would have to go down to the cave.

He settled back against the trunk of the massive tree and waited.

Eight

Rafe had plenty of time to think while he waited. He'd been trained to do this sort of thing, so he ran on autopilot, watching for any movement that was not in keeping with the lazy summer day.

It was after six, but the sun wouldn't set for a few more hours. There were some clouds forming across the hills to the south which could mean rain moving in. Rain could cool things down considerably. It might make who ever was staying there a little less wary.

He mulled over everything he'd learned since he'd arrived in Texas. Some of those things would have been better left untouched. He'd been content with his life, content with his solitude and content not needing anybody, not wanting anybody.

All of that had changed since he had returned.

Now he knew what it was to wake up with Mandy in his arms. He knew the scent of her, the taste of her. He knew the little sounds she made when she was aroused, the look of wonder on her face when she achieved her first sense of fulfillment, the feel of her arms holding him so tightly he could scarcely get his breath.

Being with her last night had been the culmination of every fantasy he'd ever dreamed since he left Texas. After this trip, he would no longer need his imagination to conjure up the experience. Memories would haunt him.

She'd made him feel things he'd never known he was capable of feeling. He didn't thank her for that. Talking about his mother and sisters last night had ripped open a wound that had long been scabbed over.

He didn't thank her for that, either.

The one thing he knew about himself above all others was that he was a survivor. He would survive this trip, as he had survived numerous wounds, raging fevers and the threat of amputation.

However, the pain would be every bit as intense.

His thoughts turned to Dan. Thinking of Dan didn't cheer him up any. Had his friend decided he could make more money smuggling computer parts out of the country than running a legitimate business?

He hoped to God that Dan wasn't doing business in that way. If he was, James Williams knew about it and was profiting from it.

But what if it was James who was involved in the theft, not Dan? And what if Dan had tried to catch the shipment before it went out? Rafe could come up with no good reason why Dan would be left alive to ever talk about it.

The occupant of the cave might be able to shed some light on what was going on out here. Now all he could do was wait to see who showed up.

Many hours later, Rafe's vigil paid off. The threatening rain had held off, but rumbles of thunder had punctuated long stretches of silence. Clouds covered most of the stars. The sliver of moon disappeared early in the evening.

He raised his night binoculars and sighted in on the moving figure, keeping the figure in sight until whoever it was went over the ridge and was no longer in view. Rafe waited another hour before quietly coming down the tree. He left his gear, knowing he could move more silently without having it accidentally brush against something.

Once on the move, he covered ground quickly. A dim light shone from the cave as he neared the opening. He took a quick peek inside, then leaned against the wall. A young boy had his back to the entrance, digging through a sack he'd brought in with him. He was alone.

Rafe stepped into the entrance of the cave and said, "Got enough food for two?"

The kid let out a shriek and whirled around, his eyes wide. As soon as he spotted Rafe, who had hunched down and was resting on his heels, he stiffened, staring at him defiantly.

"I'm not going to hurt you, you know," Rafe offered in a soothing tone. "Tell me why you're living out here in a cave, son."

The boy didn't respond. He just stood there warily watching Rafe.

He looked to be ten or thereabouts. Much too young to be out here on his own. And it was obvious he was on his own. His clothes were ragged and too small for him. His running shoes looked like someone's cast offs. His hair was shaggy, falling across his forehead and into his eyes.

Rafe was surprised that the boy looked fairly clean, as though he was making some effort to keep up his appearance. Seeing him like this had Rafe's stomach churning. It brought back too many memories.

Rafe eased down so that he was sitting on the floor of the cave. He leaned back against the wall. "You've got this fixed up really nice, you know. Hope water doesn't come in when it rains. Looks like we're going to get a gully washer before morning.''

The boy just looked at him.

Rafe sighed. ''Son, I figure that right about now you think I'm going to try to make you do something you don't want to do. You're wrong. In fact, I have a hunch, depending on how long you've been living here, that you could help me out on a matter.''

The boy shifted his weight from one foot to the other. ''How?''

He sounded so young it almost broke Rafe's heart but he knew he couldn't show his concern for the boy. He needed to get their conversation on an impersonal subject in hopes of getting him to relax.

Rafe reached into his shirt pocket and pulled out a package of jerky he'd opened earlier. He helped himself to one of the sticks, then held out the package. ''Care to join me?''

The boy looked at him suspiciously, then at the jerky. Rafe waited patiently, as though he was coaxing a hurt critter from the wild. The boy watched him. Rafe took a bite of the jerky and chewed without dropping his extended arm with his offering.

Eventually the boy inched closer until he was able to touch the package. He grabbed it and hurriedly backed away. He glanced down, then back at Rafe who still chewed. Finally the boy took one of the sticks and started to return the package.

''Keep it. I've got more.''

The boy carefully placed the remaining pieces in the pocket of his shirt.

Rafe smiled.

''What did you mean, I could help you?'' the kid finally said after they continued to eat the jerky in silence. He sat down on his bedroll, his back to the wall of the cave.

"Have you ever had a friend, somebody you played with, hung out with, did things with?"

The boy frowned. "Not anymore."

"But you've got friends like that. You know how much they mean to you, right?"

The boy looked down at his legs folded cross-legged beneath him. "Yeah," he whispered.

"That's the way Dan is. He's my friend. Dan and I have been friends since we were eight years old. That's a long time, you know...more than twenty years."

The boy kept his gaze on him. Rafe had managed to catch his interest.

"So when I got a letter from my friend a few weeks ago saying he needed my help with something, I came to find out what I could do. Because that's what friends do." Rafe looked around. "You got anything to drink? This jerky will sure make a person thirsty."

The boy scrambled up and went over to his sack. He pulled out two cans of soda pop. Showing a little less wariness, he handed one to Rafe.

"Mmm. Still cool. Thanks." He popped open the top and took a big swallow. The boy did the same once he was back on his bedroll.

"Anyway. When I got here I found my friend was gone. And nobody knows where he is. And I'm really worried about him. The last anybody knows he must have been out here because that's where they found his Jeep."

He watched closely and saw the boy give a brief nod.

"So I'm looking around, trying to figure out if I could find a clue where he might be. I happened to come across your place, and it occurred to me that you might have seen something that would help me find him."

"They shot him," the boy said in a small voice.

The words slammed into Rafe with such force that he had to pause to catch his breath. He wanted to grab the boy and shake more information out of him. Instead he drew on years of experience of learning how to become detached from his feeling in order to get a job done and force himself to appear calm.

"Who shot him?"

"I don't know."

"Can you tell me what happened?"

"I heard the Jeep drive up and I went up there along the ridge to see what it was doing there. Nobody got out, but I knew someone was there. I could see his shadow. So I watched and waited. Then I heard this airplane flying low. It circled that runway thing and then landed. It never shut down though, it just rolled to a stop and a couple of guys got out and walked over to the Jeep."

Rafe took another drink of the slightly cool cola, focused on the boy's story and not what happened to Dan.

"The guy in the Jeep got out. They all seemed to be talking at once. I heard part of what they were saying, but it didn't make any sense to me."

"Tell me what you heard."

"The men from the plane sounded like they were getting angry. The man from the Jeep just kept saying it wasn't going to happen."

"What wasn't going to happen."

"I don't know."

"He told them to go back to their boss and tell him the thing was over. He began to walk to the plane and they followed."

"Is that when they shot him?"

"No. One of them swung at him and he hit the guy, knocking him to the ground. Another guy still in the plane jumped out and pulled a gun. He shot the guy from the Jeep and he fell. The man with the gun yelled at the other two to get him in the plane. So they did."

They sat there in silence. Rafe mulled over the story. He

shouldn't be surprised but the pain in his chest was growing stronger as each minute ticked away. Now he knew why Dan hadn't contacted anyone.

"Do you think that was your friend?" the boy finally asked.

Rafe took a couple of deep breaths before he replied. "Yeah, son. That's what I think."

"I'm sorry."

"Me, too."

After a while the boy said, "I don't think it killed him, though. I think it may have hit him in the arm or shoulder, because it spun him around. And when they were moving him, I saw him lift his head. So maybe he's just hurt."

"I'd like that to be true."

"What's your name?" the boy asked.

"Rafe. What's yours?"

"Kelly."

"That's a nice name."

"So is yours."

"How long you been living here, Kelly?"

Kelly shrugged. "A while."

"How'd you find the place?"

"I was just looking for a place where there wasn't people."

"You don't care for people much, huh?"

"Not much."

"Me, either."

"Have you ever had to live in a foster home?"

Rafe thought about that one. "No, I haven't," he finally said. "How about you?"

"Once. I didn't like it."

"So you left."

"Yeah."

"What do you do for food?"

Kelly looked up at him, his blue-eyed gaze old. "I steal it."

"That can be dangerous." Rafe looked around at the things there. "You steal the sleeping bag?"

"No. It was mine. From before."

"How about clothes?"

"I don't steal clothes. Just food."

"Tough way to live."

"I don't mind."

"What if you get caught?"

Kelly shrugged.

"Have you ever thought about working on a ranch?"

Kelly blinked. "What could I do on a ranch?"

"All kinds of things. I used to work on this ranch when I wasn't much older than you."

"Really?"

"Uh-huh. I guess we have several things in common. I didn't like where I was living back then, either. So I left."

"You did?"

"Yep. I was lucky to know Dan. He owns this ranch now. When I came to work here, his mom and dad gave me a place to stay and paid me for doing work around the place. You ever thought about hiring yourself out?"

"I don't want anyone to know I'm here."

"I can certainly understand that. Here's the thing. If you decided to work and go to school, it might be arranged where you stayed here at the ranch permanently. It's not a bad place, you know."

"Are there any other kids around?"

"Nope."

"Good."

"You don't care to have kids around, huh? Guess they can be a pain sometimes."

"They steal your stuff and lie about it and nobody believes you."

"That's tough." Rafe stretched his arms high over his head and yawned. "I don't know about you, but I'm about ready for some shut-eye. Would you mind if I sleep here tonight?"

"Here?"

"Yeah. You sleep here all the time. I figure if you can do it, it probably won't bother me, either."

"I only have the sleeping bag."

"That's okay. I'm used to sleeping on the ground." Rafe stretched his length across the entrance of the cave and gave a big sigh. "I appreciate your hospitality, Kelly. I think you'd be a good friend to a person."

"You mean like Dan?"

"Uh-huh. A friend like Dan."

He closed his eyes. A few minutes later the candle went out and there was complete silence in the darkened cave. Rafe didn't want to think about Dan any more tonight. He welcomed the oblivion of sleep.

Rafe hadn't returned to the house last night and Mandy was worried. She'd kept Ranger with her as she'd promised, but he hadn't been disturbed during the night.

She'd spent a very restless night, knowing that Rafe was out in the thunderstorm that had passed through the area. She'd tried to remind herself that he had been highly trained to take care of himself. She hated to think about what he must have gone through to accumulate the various scars on his body. It would be much better not to know.

Now a second day was almost over and she still hadn't heard anything from him. She wondered if she should send Tom out to the airstrip to check on him. She didn't want to be accused of overreacting, she decided, so she looked around to find something to keep her occupied.

She'd spent yesterday cleaning the house until it shined. To give herself something to do today, she decided to make a big supper, maybe bake some cookies. She needed to do something with her time. She was going to have to call and extend her leave of absence in another couple of days. Either that, or go home.

But she didn't want to go home as long as Rafe was here. She wanted to spend whatever time she could with him. She hoped he felt the same way.

She had a large roast ready to come out of the oven when Ranger suddenly growled from where he lay sprawled by the refrigerator. Mandy eagerly peered out the window. Ranger shot toward the door, barking, which bothered her. He knew and accepted Rafe. So whoever was out there in the dark wasn't Rafe.

Only it was. She heard him speak and Ranger immediately quieted, but he still stood stiff legged and rumbled in his chest. She went to the door and opened it, saying, "Rafe?"

He stepped into the light, much as he had earlier in the week. "Yeah. It's me. I brought a new friend and we're both pretty muddy."

A new friend. What was he talking about?

"Take your boots off out there, then, and come on inside," she said. "You're just in time for a pot roast and all the trimmings. They're coming out of the oven now, but you've got time for a shower."

She was nervous and when she was nervous she chattered. Mandy didn't know what to expect. Where had Rafe been that he'd picked up a friend?

She heard the scraping of boots, and the sounds of them being removed. Rafe stepped inside and smiled at her. His eyes were wary. He stepped aside and motioned behind him.

"Mandy, I'd like you to meet Kelly." He turned to a ragamuffin of a boy and politely said, "Kelly, this is Mandy, the woman I told you about. She's Dan's sister."

The boy looked too thin. His eyes seemed to cover half

his face. He had the biggest, bluest eyes she'd ever seen. His hair was sandy blond with darker strands mixed in and it didn't look as if it had come into contact with shampoo in a while. He was watching her as if he thought she would immediately order him out of the house.

He was breaking her heart.

"I'm very pleased to meet you, Kelly. Any friend of Rafe's is a friend of mine. We have two showers, so if you'd like to get cleaned up before supper, you can."

Kelly looked at Rafe. Rafe nodded and said, "Sounds good to me. I'll show you where everything is." He gently placed his hand on the boy's shoulder and the two of them walked out of the kitchen together.

What in the world was going on? Mandy knew that sooner or later Rafe would explain, but for now, Kelly's appearance was a definite mystery. Since all the vehicles were still parked here at the ranch buildings, she knew Rafe hadn't left the property unless he walked, which she doubted.

So how had he found Kelly?

She hurried to her room and went to the back of her large walk-in closet. She remembered packing a box of old clothes—some jeans and Western shirts she'd worn before she moved away from home. They were too small for her now, but she hadn't wanted to throw them out, and hadn't taken the time to drop them off at the local thrift store.

Most of the stuff was unisex. She dumped out the box and pawed through the clothing, laying out what she hoped would be suitable. She sat back on her heels. She didn't have any underwear for him and anything of Dan's or Rafe's would be too big. She shook her head. At least these clothes would be an improvement over the ones he wore now.

She stopped at the hall bathroom and tapped on the door. There was a tense silence before Kelly answered.

"Yes?" he answered, sounding a little unnerved.

"I found some things you can put on when you get done so we can wash what you're wearing, if you'd like."

She waited while he thought about that. Slowly he opened the door and looked out. She handed them to him. He looked at her, at the clothes, back at her. "Thank you," he finally said.

She smiled. "They'll probably be too big for you, but at least they're clean."

As soon as he shut the door she hurried down to the bath in the master bedroom. Rafe was already in the shower. Well, that was just too bad. She wanted some answers and didn't want to ask them in front of the boy.

She opened the bathroom door and stepped inside. He had his head under the water, scrubbing it, and didn't hear her come in. She waited until he rinsed his hair and was soaping his body when she asked, "What's going on, Rafe?"

He spun around. When he saw her standing there he grinned at her. "Care to join me?"

When he looked at her like that, it was hard to keep her mind on the matter at hand. "I want to know where you found Kelly."

"Living in a cave near the landing strip."

"Oh my God."

"Yeah."

"Who is he?"

"I have no idea. But I've convinced him to trade places with me for a while."

"What do you mean, trade places?"

"I'll tell you over supper. But in the meantime, I've practically promised him a job on the ranch. Do you think Tom can use him?"

"How would I know? He's just a little boy."

"Well, you and Dan worked around here at his age. So

there must be something he can do to earn his keep. Because I sure don't want him sleeping down there anymore.''

"Well, neither do I." She was having a really hard time concentrating on their conversation while watching Rafe rinse the soap from his body. She had to fight the urge to run her hands over his muscled exterior to make sure he was all right. She'd missed him terribly after only two days and a night. This did not bode well for her future without him.

He turned off the water and reached for a towel. She got it first. "Allow me," she said and soon matched actions with words. When she saw how he responded to her touch, she smiled.

"Well, hell, Mandy. What did you expect?" he groused, a little embarrassed. "I'm not used to having a woman's hands on me without getting ready to do something about it."

"Do you hear me complaining?"

"No, but—"

"No, but nothing. Get dressed so we can eat while it's hot." She practically ran from the room before she did something that would embarrass her. Somehow she was going to have to learn some control around this man.

She caught herself grinning like a fool while she dished up their meal.

Mandy had all the food on the table—place settings and glasses neatly arranged—when Kelly appeared in the doorway. She paused from filling the glasses with water and smiled at him. "Ready to eat?" she asked.

As she had guessed, the clothes were too large. He'd rolled up the jeans' legs and used his belt to gather the waist in. The cuffs on the shirt were rolled up. The large opening at the throat emphasized his delicate neck. She wanted to gather him up in her arms and hug him, but of course she couldn't, even though she knew the child was in dire need of one.

"Where's Rafe?" he asked, looking around the room as though she'd hidden him away somewhere.

"Getting cleaned up, like you." She pointed to one of the chairs. "Have a seat. Would you like some milk?"

He eyed her, the chair, the table filled with food, then looked back at her with suspicion. "Who else is coming?"

"You, me and Rafe. Why?"

"That's a lot of food for three people."

She grinned. "I got carried away. But it makes good leftovers."

Mandy was relieved when Rafe appeared behind the boy. He casually dropped his hand on the boy's shoulder. "Feels good to get into some clean clothes, doesn't it?" he asked, gently guiding Kelly to the table.

Kelly sat down next to Rafe and unobtrusively scooted his chair closer to him. Rafe pretended not to notice. It was a good thing Rafe was left-handed, Mandy thought, hiding a smile. He wouldn't be able to use his right hand or arm without jostling the boy.

Mandy wasn't sure what she could say or do to make the boy more comfortable. Once he saw that they were filling their plates with generous portions, Kelly did, too. She noticed that he waited to see what the others did each time before attempting to eat.

They were midway through their meal before the stiffness began to leave Kelly's spine. He leaned back in his chair and offered her a big grin. "You're a good cook, Mandy. This stuff is great."

"Yeah, that's what I keep telling her," Rafe said. His grin was filled with mischief.

Unable to contain her curiosity a moment longer, Mandy asked Kelly, "Isn't your mother worried about you being gone so long?"

Well, you would have thought she'd suggested the two guys at the table star in a porno film, the way they froze. All right, so maybe she shouldn't have brought it up, but darn it! Kelly was such a cutie. It was obvious that someone had taught him some manners. So where was she now?

Rafe shot her a riveting frown as though she'd showed a lamentable breach in good manners, herself. It wasn't as if they were still living in the Old West where no one was supposed to ask questions about a person's past. Besides, Kelly was just a child. He had absolutely no business being on his own.

Rafe continued to eat. Kelly drank some milk. Finally he blurted out, "She died."

"Oh," Mandy replied. "I'm so sorry, Kelly. It's really tough to lose your mom. My mom died, too. I really miss her."

He nodded. "Yeah. She got pneumonia, but that's not supposed to kill ya. But the doctor who finally saw her said she was all run-down and amenic and stuff."

"Anemic?"

"Where she doesn't have enough blood or something," he explained.

"I see." Mandy met Rafe's glare with a slight nod of acknowledgment that she knew he disapproved of her questions, all the while she continued to probe. "How long ago did she die?"

Kelly shrugged. "A long time. Last year, sometime."

"Yes. That *is* a long time."

As though forestalling her next question, Kelly said, "I don't have a dad. It was just me and Mom. Mom did cleaning for people and worked in a convenience store, and did these different jobs all the time so we could stay together. She didn't want anybody to take me away from her."

"She sounds like a wonderful mom."

Kelly's face lit up. "She was! She was my best pal." He looked at Rafe. "My best friend," he added, soberly.

Rafe nodded but made it clear he wasn't part of the conversation by concentrating on his food.

Now that the dam had been broken, Kelly opened up. "Rafe says that maybe I could get a job working on your ranch. I'm a real good worker. He also told me he'd like to borrow my place for a while and that I could stay here in his place. You know, like a trade." He glanced at Rafe to be sure he was giving her the straight scoop.

Rafe smiled at him. "That's right. I figure we'll sleep here tonight. I'll talk to Tom in the morning, then while I'm sleeping at Kelly's place, he can stay here with you for now."

"I've got to make friends with your dog, though," Kelly solemnly explained to her.

All three of them looked over at Ranger who still zealously guarded the refrigerator. "I don't think you'll have any problem with that," Mandy said around the lump in her throat.

Rafe McClain could be the roughest, toughest, meanest person around. He could also offer a homeless child hope and a promise for a better future. If she didn't already love him to distraction, his treatment of Kelly would have knocked out all her defenses against him.

Rafe cleared his throat. He had a clean plate in front of him. He drained his glass of milk. "Kelly has been a big help to me," he began, cupping Kelly's nape and gently massaging. "I think I've come up with a workable plan to find Dan."

Mandy stared at him. "And you're just now telling me about it?"

He motioned to his plate. "First things first. I'm telling you now. You have a problem with that?"

She sighed. "Go on."

"Well, Kelly tells me that there are a couple of planes landing on the strip on a regular basis. He's watched them and noticed that the first plane unloads some things and hides them nearby. Within a couple of nights the other plane lands and they leave something and take what's there. It's the first plane that I'm interested in. It's the one Dan left in."

"Oh, Rafe." She looked at Kelly. "So you saw my brother the night he left! Oh, that's wonderful."

Kelly looked at Rafe before nodding his head.

"I figure that somebody set up a nice little operation using that landing strip. Probably doesn't have anything to do with Dan. There's a strong possibility the strip was spotted from the air, checked out and was commandeered because of its accessibility and relative privacy."

"Do you know where Dan is?"

"Not yet, but I'm going to find out. I'm going to wait out there until the first plane shows up with a drop. Then I intend to hitch a ride with them, much like Dan did, and see what I can find out."

Mandy eyed him uncertainly. "Won't that be dangerous? These people are obviously doing something illegal. Can't you just call the sheriff and have them picked up?"

"I could. Eventually I intend to do just that. But I want to find Dan first. Once they're in custody, they won't talk about Dan, I guarantee you."

"Oh. So you think they're holding him somewhere?"

"That's what I intend to find out."

"What if they decide to hold you, too?"

The smile he gave her made her shiver. "They can try." He looked at Kelly. "So I've asked Kelly if he'll stay here and help Ranger look after you while I'm gone, since I don't know how long this is going to take. I'll talk to Tom in the morning about Kelly's assignments." He met Mandy's gaze and held it. "I figured you could use the company."

"Yes," she managed to say. What else could she say? This was Rafe in his most in-charge-of-things attitude. Not that she minded having Kelly there. It beat living in a cave, of all things. Rafe was right. She could use the company. She needed the distraction—first from worrying about Dan, second from worrying about Rafe.

"Is Dan's old room available, the one he used when he was a kid?"

"It's become a storage room more than a bedroom these past few years." She smiled at Kelly. "If you don't mind the ruffles on the curtains, you can sleep in the room I used when I was growing up." Since that was the same room she had been sleeping in since her return, Rafe lifted one brow at her in silent inquiry.

She returned his look with a sunny smile.

When she glanced at Kelly she could see he was already nodding off. A full tummy can do that to a person. She stood and began to gather plates. "Why don't you get him bedded down while I clean up the kitchen, okay?"

"Well, I thought maybe you'd want to do that, since it's your room."

"Oh, I'll get whatever I need out of there later."

Kelly looked like it was taking a great deal of effort for him to keep his eyes open. Rafe got up and assisted Kelly. "Come on, sport. Time to hit the sack."

As soon as she finished in the kitchen, Mandy went looking for Rafe. She found him in the den watching the late-night news.

"Is he okay?" she asked, sitting next to him on the couch.

"He was asleep by the time his head hit the pillow. I think we've managed to win over his trust and when he let down his guard, his body caved. He's probably been running on adrenaline for a long time."

"Did you find out how old he is?" she asked.

"He says he's twelve, but I don't believe it. Ten, maybe. Eleven is stretching it. But twelve? No way."

"Did he say why he's living out like this?"

"I think he ran away from a foster situation."

"People are looking for him, you know."

Rafe gave her what she always thought of as "the look."

"Now you're sounding like part of Children's Services."

"What a surprise."

"If you want to find out something on him while I'm gone, be my guest."

"He's got to be in school in September, Rafe. You know that."

"I know you'll do whatever you think is best."

"Yes," she said with a nod. "I will."

"Why did you give up your room? We could have found him someplace else to sleep."

"Because my room is ready for him and he was ready to crash. Besides, I already have a place to sleep."

"Oh, yeah? Where's that?"

"With you."

Nine

"Uh, Mandy, I don't think that's a good idea."

"Probably not," she admitted, "but what the hell, I'll pay the price later." She leaned toward him and kissed his jawline. "In the meantime, I'm going to spend whatever time I can with you. Hang the consequences."

"You know there's never going to be a long-term relationship between us. We're too different...my work takes me halfway around the world—it would never work between us."

Mandy studied him for a long moment, reading more than he probably wanted her to see in his expression. She smiled. "Let's see now," she said, holding up her fingers. Pointing to the index finger, she said, "*A*, whether you like it or not, Rafe, we've been in a long-term relationship since we were kids." She saw him flinch at the statement, but he made no attempt to contradict her. Feeling a little more confident, she pointed to her second finger and said, "*B*, yes we are very different from each other. I, personally, don't have a problem with that. Sorry if you do." She gave him a quick kiss then pointed to her ring finger and said, "And C, I've never seen you as a nine-to-five guy in my wildest dreams, cowboy. You are who you are. You do what you feel compelled to do. I would never try to change you." She tilted her head at him and smiled.

He sighed as though carrying a tremendous weight on his shoulders. "You didn't mention the most important part— it will never work between us."

"Not if you don't want it to. But it's working now, tonight, for the next few hours. I'm willing to accept that, even if there's no more. Whether you want to admit it to me or not, what you're planning to do is exceedingly dangerous. You've got a good chance of getting yourself killed. Even worse, I may never know for sure. You're planning to disappear in the same way Dan did, and it could turn out to be with the same results."

"Which is my point. I don't want to hurt you in any way. That's the last thing I want."

"I'm a big girl now, Rafe. I told you that. I'm no longer fifteen."

"Or innocent," he added with a wicked gleam.

"I should say not, considering all the things you did to me the other night."

"With you, not to you," he whispered. "We did them together."

She draped her arms around his shoulders. "Care to show me another demonstration?" She lightly kissed him, then pulled away to watch his expression.

"Damn, woman, I've never been able to resist you."

"Then don't start trying to at this late date," she replied. She rose and held out her hand. He stood and lightly grasped her wrist between his thumb and index finger while she led him down the hall to the master bedroom.

* * *

When Tom Parker stepped out of his house early the next morning he found Rafe sitting on his porch steps. "You're out and about early," Tom said. "Did you have any luck looking around the landing strip?"

Rafe stood and Tom joined him on the steps. In unspoken agreement, they started toward the other ranch buildings. "I know how Dan left the ranch. I intend to do the same thing in hopes of finding him."

"How did you manage that?"

"I found a kid living down there. His name is Kelly and I think I've convinced him that you could find work for him to do around here."

"That's for sure. How old is he?"

"Ten or eleven is my guess. No telling what he'll tell you. Twenty-one if he thought you'd believe him."

"A runaway?"

"That's a given. Knowing Mandy, she'll have all his credentials and his history by the time I get back." He glanced at Tom, then away. "I hope you'll be able to use him. He needs looking after, despite what he thinks. He needs clothes, shoes, you name it. But he has to earn the money himself, so don't even try to offer him cash."

"Sounds like you know him pretty well."

"I've known him all my life."

"Is the kid yours?" Tom asked.

Rafe laughed. "Not with that blond hair and blue eyes. But I understand him. If you give him a chance, he'll work his heart out for you."

"Send him out and I'll put him to work."

Rafe held out his hand. "Thanks, Tom. I owe you one."

Tom shook his head. "You don't owe me a thing. But I'd sure appreciate your bringing the boss home. We need him around here."

"I'll see what I can do."

Rafe had cautioned Kelly not to tell anyone that Dan had

been shot. He saw no reason to upset Mandy, especially, when no one at this point knew how serious the wound was. There was time enough later to fill her in on all of the events once he could be with her to deal with the news.

When Rafe slipped back into the house, he found Mandy making coffee. She glanced at him, then concentrated on the coffee. "I woke up and found you gone. I didn't think I'd see you again this morning."

"I needed to talk with Tom. He said he'd find Kelly plenty to do around here."

"That's good."

He walked over to her and put his arms around her waist. "I'm sorry, Mandy."

"For what?"

"For not being the type of man you want me to be...the kind of man you need—one who doesn't keep disappearing on you."

She turned in his arms. "You have nothing to apologize for. Nothing. I'm glad you decided to respond to Dan's message and came back to Texas. I hope you locate Dan, but even if you don't, your visit has been so good for me."

"I'll find him, Mandy. I'm glad I came back, too, for many reasons. I feel as though I allowed my past to become a raging tiger that I never wanted to face. I'm discovering that, by confronting it, the tiger has become a tabby kitten, nothing so ferocious or dangerous after all."

He heard a soft footfall nearby and looked around. Kelly stood in the doorway. As promised, Mandy had washed and dried his clothes and he now wore them. Even clean, they were pretty disreputable, but they were his.

Rafe understood.

"I figure we'll have some breakfast and then go out and talk to the foreman. That sound okay?"

Kelly grinned. "Yeah. I mean, yes, sir."

"Practicing, are you?"

"My mom says, uh, said, that politeness is never out of place."

"I agree," Rafe said, pouring himself a cup of the freshly brewed coffee. He went over to the table and sat down. Kelly joined him. Mandy poured them both some orange juice, plus filled a glass with milk for Kelly. "Breakfast will be ready shortly."

By midafternoon Kelly was running from barn to tool-shed, from tractor to backhoe. Rafe had never heard so many questions coming out of one person's mouth. It took both of them—he and Tom—to attempt to supply answers and there were times when they were both stumped.

Eventually Rafe left Kelly with Tom and went back to the house. When he found Mandy, he said, "I'm going to get a few hours of sleep, then I'll go on down to the strip. I'll take the Jeep, but make sure it's hidden from the air. Once they land, it won't matter if they spot it."

"Do you expect them tonight?"

"There's no way to know. Kelly didn't note the nights they showed up, but he said they came regularly and he hadn't seen them in a while. I'm hoping to get lucky. Maybe they'll show up tonight."

However, it was four nights later when Rafe heard the sound of a single-engine plane coming in low. During the days he'd returned to the house and visited with Kelly and Mandy, eaten, slept and returned to the airstrip at sunset. He had enjoyed seeing the bond that Kelly was forming with both Tom and Mandy. As much as it pained him to know that he wouldn't be a part of their lives, he felt good knowing that Tom would be there for them.

Now he scrambled to the top of the gully and watched as the plane circled before preparing to land. When the plane turned away from where he was, he slid over the rim and moved into the position he'd chosen earlier.

He had done as much preparing as he could for this mission. He'd dismissed every thought but the need to get into that plane alive. He'd focused on each step to ensure the success of that goal. It felt good, finally, to be going into action.

Kelly had shown him where the drop was. It was almost too easy to step behind the man as he turned away from leaving an attaché case in the Y of a tree. He caught him in a grip that included a knife at his throat.

"You're going to be just fine," he said in a low voice directly into the man's ear, "so long as you cooperate with me. We're going back to the plane. Whether both of us get on is up to you. I intend to be on board. Understand?"

The man shivered and gave a brief nod.

"Good."

As soon as they reached the plane, one of the men inside said, "What's going on?"

Rafe replied. "Just hitching a ride, my friend."

No one said anything when he lifted the man in front of him into the plane and climbed in behind him. Maybe it was the camouflage uniform. Or it could have been the blacking on his face. It might even have been the combat knife he still held.

"Let's go," he said, tapping the pilot's shoulder with the knife blade.

No one argued with him.

Once strapped in, Rafe looked around the interior of the plane. There were two men seated in front. He and his newest companion were in back. The three kept darting glances his way.

Probably wanted to know the name of his fashion consultant.

"What do you want?" the passenger in the front seat said once they were in the air and had leveled off.

"I hate to sound like a cliche, but the truth is—I want you to take me to your leader."

"Why?"

"My reasons don't concern you."

"He ain't going to be happy to see you."

"I'll try to bear up under the disappointment."

Rafe watched the ground below. There wasn't much light, but at least there was no cloud cover. The stars looked close enough to touch.

During the time he had waited in the cave, he studied aerial maps of the area between the ranch and the border. He was pleased to see that he was right. They were crossing the border and flying into the interior of Mexico.

So far, so good.

When they finally landed at another small airstrip hours later, he noted there were landing lights and a hangar nearby, but no one waiting for them on the ground. After the landing, they taxied up to the hangar and the pilot cut the engine.

"Now what?" their spokesman asked.

"Now we go see The Man."

"He's asleep by now."

"No problem. I'll add to his pleasant dreams."

The men looked at each other, then shrugged.

Rafe knew they were armed. He also knew that if they tried anything, he could take two of them out if he was lucky. The odds didn't bother him.

He let the men lead the way into what appeared to be a large hacienda nestled in the mountains. The pilot said, "I'm going to bed. You wanna kill me, go ahead."

Rafe almost smiled. "Sleep well, *amigo*."

The pilot looked at him in surprise, then shrugged and disappeared into the darkness. Of course he could be planning to come up behind Rafe and disarm him. Rafe was willing to take that chance.

Once inside the hacienda the two remaining men looked at each other. One of them said, "We wake him up, *he'll* kill us."

The other nodded toward Rafe. "We don't wake him up, he'll kill us."

"May I make a suggestion, gentlemen?" Rafe asked politely.

They looked at him.

"Tell me where to find him. He'll never need to know how I got here."

They looked at him, then each other. The spokesman gave directions while the other took off out the front door. As soon as he finished with the directions, the spokesman followed his friend.

Interesting loyalties.

Rafe climbed the stairs two at a time, went down the broad hallway and paused at the double doors at the end. He tried the door. It silently gave to the pressure and swung open.

Rafe stepped inside and closed the door behind him.

The room had windows on three sides that let in the dim light. The bed was on a large dais in the middle of the room.

From the looks of things, the boss man slept alone. At least tonight.

He woke up quickly enough, Rafe noticed, which was good. He seemed to be alert, although he didn't have much to say. It could be because of the cold steel caressing his carotid artery.

Once Rafe was certain he had the man's attention, he said, "I won't take up much of your time. I'm looking for a friend of mine. Dan Crenshaw."

The man blinked.

"Uh-huh. Dan. I've come for him. So here's the plan. You take me to him, you put us on the plane you've got sitting out there and you fly us across the border. *¿Comprende?*"

Rafe could now see the whites of the man's eyes. That's because his gaze kept darting around the room. "You want me to spell it out a little clearer for you?" Rafe asked, putting pressure on the blade.

How amazing. The man's eyes were downright eloquent. He didn't need to say a word to convince Rafe he wanted to cooperate in the worst way.

Rafe removed his knee from the man's chest and eased back. "Get up."

The man leaped out of bed.

"Take me to Dan."

The man looked down at his nudity. Rafe spotted a pair of trousers draped over a chair. He tossed them to him and kicked a pair of huaraches, a sandal common to Mexico, toward him.

Damned if he didn't act grateful.

"Lead the way," Rafe said. The man looked at him as though he was dealing with a crazy person. He wasn't far off at the moment. Rafe's blood was pumping and so was his adrenaline. His perceptions were heightened and he was more than ready to take someone out.

The man must have sensed Rafe's mood, or, like his henchmen, was dazzled by his fashion sense, because he made no argument. Instead he headed toward the door.

Rafe walked a step behind the man down the hallway and stairs. There were no guards waiting downstairs. They turned when they reached the bottom and walked toward the back of the hacienda. The man went through a door that opened onto a large patio filled with all kinds of blooming flowers and shrubs.

The man walked faster through an archway built into the adobe wall around the place. He followed a graveled path that wound through the trees. Rafe could see small cottages among the trees, no doubt where the workers lived.

The man kept looking over his shoulder as though to make certain Rafe was behind him. Maybe he hoped he was just having a really scary nightmare and would wake up at any moment.

When the man paused, Rafe almost stepped on him. The pause was to open a wrought iron gate. Rafe looked around and realized where they were.

He'd been brought to the family cemetery.

Ten

Rafe wanted to scream with rage. He grabbed the man, ready to slit his throat for what he had done to Dan. He forced himself to hang on, searching for some self-control deep inside.

Yes, he'd known the chances were good that Dan hadn't survived the gunshot wound. But he hadn't wanted to believe it.

I came as fast as I got your message, he said to Dan in his head. *Why did you have to try to play the role of hero? Why couldn't you have waited for me? You knew I was coming, damn you. You knew that I wouldn't ignore your summons. If you'd waited two more weeks we could have done this together with a different outcome.*

He still wasn't going to leave him here. He had come to bring Dan home and he was going to do it, if he had to dig with his bare hands.

Slowly he unclenched his fingers from the man's neck.

The man hurried along the pathway inside the cemetery and Rafe numbly followed him. No wonder nobody argued with him on this trip. Hell, it hadn't mattered. Dead men don't talk.

Rafe heard the sound of another gate opening before he understood that the man he followed had opened the second gate, the one leading out of the cemetery, and was continuing down the path.

What the hell was going on? Rafe glanced over his shoulder. They had followed the most direct route from the hacienda, which happened to be through the family's resting place.

He picked up his pace. Was it possible that he had misunderstood? Please, God, let it be so.

They must have walked close to a mile before the path led them to an isolated cottage in the woods. The man pounded on the door and called out in Spanish.

A match flared inside and an oil lamp was lit. An old woman, her gray hair streaming around her shoulders, answered the door. She stared at them with a wide, frightened gaze.

The man said something low that Rafe didn't hear. The woman nodded vigorously several times, then opened the door wider. Rafe motioned the man to enter ahead of him. Once inside, he found himself in a two-room cottage, sparsely furnished. There was a bed in the far corner of the room he had entered. The woman walked over to it, holding the lamp high so that he could see.

Dan Crenshaw lay there, a sheet pulled up to his waist, his chest bare except for the bandage wrapped around it. His shoulder was also bandaged, but the white dressings couldn't hide the inflammation radiating around the wound.

"You've left him this way for weeks? Can't you see the damn wound's infected? It wasn't enough to shoot him, you have to let him die by degrees?" He touched Dan's forehead, unsurprised to feel the heat. He was burning with fever.

"You're going to help me carry this man to the plane," he said to the man beside him. "If you try anything, I'll kill you, do you understand?"

The man nodded.

Rafe began to question the woman in Spanish. She rattled off her answers. She had tried to care for the man. She'd removed the bullet, tried to cleanse the wound, but sometimes infections occur, no matter what you do. She had kept him fed, changed his dressings, made him herbal teas. She had done all she could.

Rafe motioned for the man to sit down in the chair beside the bed so he could see him. He sat on the edge of the bed and took Dan's hand. "Is this any way to greet me, good buddy?" he asked. "What the hell were you thinking, anyway? Did you forget which one of us was the Commando, which one the Harvard grad?"

He checked Dan's pulse. It was light and racing, but by damn he had one.

Rafe could work with that.

He tucked the sheet around Dan and motioned for the man to help him. Between the two of them they lifted him from the bed. The old woman hurried to the door and held it open for them. Rafe shouldered his way through, careful not to jar Dan any more than he had to. Every step of the way back to the hacienda Rafe prayed that God would spare Dan's life. He had kept him alive this long. Dan was a fighter. Always had been. If anyone could pull through, Dan would.

Both of the men were breathing hard when they reached the hacienda. For the first time since Rafe had arrived, the man spoke to him.

"We can put him down here while I go for the plane." He motioned to the chaise lounge on the patio.

Once they had stretched Dan out, the man stepped back. "I'm going with you," Rafe said. "You and I are going to get that plane. You'll have your men *carefully* bring him to the plane. If anything goes wrong, know that you won't live to see the sun, amigo."

"If I wanted him dead, he would already be dead," the man said, turning his back on Rafe. Rafe grabbed the man's arm and lifted it high on his back.

"Why didn't you bring him home?"

"I planned to, when he got better."

"You know him?"

"Yes."

"You've been doing business with him?"

"I thought so, until he was shot. He was not the man I knew as Dan Crenshaw. I never saw this man before, but his identification showed me that I had been misled."

"But you were still intending to let him go, huh? Out of the kindness of your heart?"

"I do not deal in violence, despite what you think. The man who shot your friend no longer works for me."

"Aren't you afraid of what Dan can tell us about you?"

The man tried to straighten, but the arm hold kept him bent. "No one can prove anything about me or my business. We are in Mexico. Your authorities have no jurisdiction over me."

"So you're feeling safe enough."

"If not, you would have been dead before you stepped into my plane tonight."

"So you know how I got here?"

"Don't make the mistake of thinking me stupid."

Rafe released his arm. The man rubbed his shoulder. "On second thought, let's you and I take Dan on to the plane. I think it would be a good idea for you to fly back with us."

"That isn't necessary."

"I think it is."

"If you think you can hold me there, you are wrong."

"I'm not interested in anything but getting Dan back to Texas. I just want a little insurance that we'll make it there. You being in the plane gives me a better sense of safety, somehow. You'll be my security blanket."

The man shrugged and returned to Dan's side. Once again they lifted him and followed the path to the landing strip. No one was there when they arrived. The plane was empty.

"Do you know how to fly this thing?" The man nodded. "Then let's get Dan in the back and get it ready. You'll need more fuel." He watched the man go through the pre-flight check. They got into the plane and taxied over to where the fuel supply was.

It was while they were refueling that Dan finally stirred and opened his eyes. He stared at Rafe watching him from the front seat of the cockpit without blinking.

"So you finally decided to wake up and join the party, huh?"

Dan closed his eyes for a moment, then opened them again. "Rafe?" he whispered. He lifted his hand as though to touch Rafe's face.

Rafe grinned. "Yep, it's me under all this paint."

"Thought I'd died and gone to hell," Dan mumbled.

"Our host has agreed to fly us out of here. You ready to go home?"

Dan nodded and closed his eyes.

So was Rafe.

The sun had been up several hours by the time the plane landed at the ranch. Rafe hadn't said anything more to the man who had flown them there. He felt that they both understood each other without further communication.

By the time the plane stopped rolling, Rafe had the door open. He lifted Dan out and started running toward the Jeep without looking back. By the time the plane took off, Rafe had Dan in the back of the Jeep. He headed back to the house, his foot on the accelerator and pressed to the floor.

Tom must have seen him flying over the last hill as he approached the house because he was standing in the driveway when Rafe came barreling up.

As soon as Rafe braked beside him and he saw Dan in the back seat, Tom said, "My God, you did it." He sounded incredulous.

"He's got to have immediate medical help. Take him to the nearest hospital while I go get cleaned up. I'll follow as soon as I can." He leaped out of the Jeep and sprinted toward the house.

Tom yelled the name of the nearest hospital and where it was located and Rafe waved without stopping. When he reached the house, he slowed down and walked in calmly.

His restraint was wasted. No one was there.

He hit the shower and scrubbed the paint off his face. Within minutes he was dressed and ready to leave. He took time to leave a note for Mandy, then took off in his borrowed truck.

By the time Rafe got to the hospital, they had admitted Dan. Tom waited in the hall for him, a grin on his face. "They're pumping him full of antibiotics, they've cleaned out the wound and done some fancy dressings, and they've got him on a drip to rehydrate him."

"What do they say about his chances?"

"Nobody's saying. They're just working on him, doing what they do best."

"Did he ever come to?"

Tom's grin widened. "Yeah. He recognized me. Looked surprised to see me. Then asked if he'd been hallucinating or whether you were actually here."

Rafe laughed out loud. "Yeah, I think I scared the religion out of him, or into him, I'm not sure which." He looked around the hallway. "I could use a cup of coffee. Do you know where I could find one?"

"Yeah. Unfortunately I've had to come in here on a disgustingly regular basis. Somebody's always getting hurt and needing to be patched up." Tom took him to the cafeteria where they were able to get coffee and Rafe some breakfast.

"By the way," Rafe said, once they were seated, "Where are Mandy and Kelly? I didn't see either one of them when I was at the house."

Tom shook his head. "That little guy didn't know what he was in for when Mandy got a hold of him."

"Yeah? What happened?"

"She's been getting bits and pieces of information out of him all week. Did she tell you?"

"No. We haven't had much of a chance to talk. If I wasn't asleep he was right there catching me up on his day and Mandy hadn't mentioned anything about his past to me. So what's been going on?"

"She finally got him to tell her where he and his mother lived, then managed to get in touch with Children's Services and got all the rest of the information she needed. She's already talking about petitioning for custody of him. She was told that, with her background, she wouldn't have any problem getting temporary custody, although she'll be taking him back to Dallas with her eventually."

"So they're dealing with paperwork this morning?"

"Nope. They were getting an early start on shopping."

"Shopping?"

"Yep. She informed Master Kelly that he had to look like he was cared for and loved and that she was taking him shopping whether he liked it or not. She also found out that he had a birthday last week—you were right…he just turned eleven—and she convinced him that most of what they were going to buy was going to be birthday presents. The rest he could pay out of his wages."

"I see."

"She's a formidable lady."

"That she is."

"So what are you going to do about her?"

Rafe had finished his food and was now reaching for his coffee when he froze with his hand halfway to the cup. "Me? I'm not in charge of the woman." He took a sip of the coffee and sighed. "Thank God."

"She's in love with you," Tom said.

Damn, but the man liked to be blunt.

"No she's not. We've just been friends for a long time."

"I've known her for a long time as well. I see the way she looks at you, the way she talks about you. I know what I'm seeing."

Rafe shook his head. "Whatever you're thinking, it's wrong. Can you see me a married man?" He laughed, even if it did sound a little hollow. "And now she's asking for custody of Kelly. She needs to find a good father figure, an example for kids. That's not me."

"Whatever you say."

"Come on. I want to go check on Dan."

The hospital staff finally let him in to see Dan a couple of hours later after reassuring him that Dan was responding satisfactorily to the medications. When he walked in, Dan was asleep. Rafe didn't care. He would sit there for a while and look at his friend…his living, breathing friend. That was good enough for him.

He sat down in the large, upholstered chair beside the bed and rested his head against the back. Dan's color was already better, his breathing eased. The marvels of modern technology, he thought, had saved Dan's life. He would have died in that little Mexican cottage for lack of antibiotics readily available here.

Another day, maybe two at the most, and the medical

profession might not have been able to bring him around. Rafe recognized his reaction for what it was. He went through the shakes after every mission, successful or not. This one had been particularly difficult because he'd had to concentrate on keeping his focus on the job he'd set for himself.

He'd lost his concentration for a time in that cemetery. He closed his eyes. Yeah, he'd lost more than his concentration. He'd almost killed the man he held responsible. He smiled grimly to himself. For that moment in time, the mission had become extremely personal to him.

Rafe didn't realize he'd drifted off to sleep until several hours later when he heard Mandy's voice. He opened his eyes and found her hanging over Dan's bed, hugging him. "Oh, Dan, I can't believe it. I was so afraid you were dead."

Rafe stretched and stood so that he was on the other side of Dan's bed. Dan spotted him and held out his hand. "You can thank this guy that I'm not," Dan said to Mandy. "At least, that's what they tell me. I'm afraid I don't remember much about it."

Mandy glanced at Rafe, then back at Dan. "What happened to you? Why are you in the hospital?"

"Oh, a minor wound got infected, that's all," Dan replied. He looked from one to the other. "I can't believe you're both here. Hell, I can't believe I'm in an Austin hospital. Nobody's bothered to tell me how I got here from some little room in the mountains somewhere."

Mandy smiled at Rafe. "Rafe found you and brought you back."

"Still playing the hero these days, are you?" Dan said, squeezing Rafe's hand. Rafe could feel the tremor that denoted how weak Dan was.

"When did you get here, Mandy?" Dan asked. "I

thought you weren't going to take your vacation until next month.''

"Do you really think I could work when nobody seemed to know what had happened to you? I've been staying at the ranch for the past week or so."

"What did you do, get a hold of Rafe and tell him I'd disappeared?"

"She didn't have to. Your letter finally caught up with me. I got here as soon as I could. Obviously not soon enough."

Dan gazed at him as though he still found it hard to believe Rafe was there. "I'm glad you're here."

"Me, too."

"Dan," Mandy said, "there's somebody waiting out in the hall who wants to meet you. Would you mind if I bring him in?"

"I don't mind. Don't tell me you got yourself engaged again. Man, if I don't keep an eye on you every minute, you get in some of the craziest situations."

She dropped her gaze to her folded hands. "Well, actually, I *have* asked him to live with me."

Dan rolled his eyes. "For God's sake, Mandy, when are you going to learn not to step in over your head? How long have you known him, anyway?"

"Not long. In fact, Rafe introduced us."

Dan looked at both of them as though convinced they'd lost their collective mind. "I thought better of you, Rafe. I really did. In my absence, you should have been looking after her, not encouraging her to go off the deep end."

Rafe still held Dan's hand. He patted it and said, "I really think you need to meet him before you start making all these judgments about him."

"Yeah, fine. Bring him in," Dan said, frowning.

Mandy went to the door and leaned out. She signaled and came back in the room, smiling.

Rafe did a double take when Kelly appeared in the doorway. He'd gotten a haircut since Rafe had seen him, almost military in appearance. He wore a chambray shirt, new jeans and a pair of cowboy boots. He saw Rafe and hurried over to him. "Look at my boots, Rafe. Mandy got them for me for my birthday."

"They're pretty sharp, son. You look like you're ready to throw your leg over a pony any time."

"Tom said he'd teach me to ride, but right now I have to learn how to take care of a horse first." He looked up at Dan. "Hi." Suddenly he was shy.

Rafe took over. "Dan, I want you to meet Kelly. He's the one who told me where you were. If it hadn't've been for Kelly, I'm afraid I wouldn't have found you at all."

Dan had been staring at Kelly in amazement since he'd walked in the room. He took turns staring at first Mandy and then Rafe. He shook his head. "Okay, guys. You suckered me in on that one."

"You did it to yourself, Dan," Mandy replied. "You were the one jumping to conclusions. We just gave you more room to keep leaping."

"So you're Kelly," Dan said. "I'm glad to meet you." He held out his hand, which happened to be his left, and Kelly took it and gingerly shook it.

"I saw them shoot you," he said in a small voice.

"What?" Mandy exclaimed. "You were shot? And nobody told me?"

Dan replied. "It wasn't serious until infection set in. I'm going to be okay."

She looked at Kelly. "You knew and you never told me?"

Rafe spoke up. He could see the anger and confusion in her eyes. "I told him not to mention it, Mandy. There was no reason to upset you at that point."

Dan returned his gaze to Kelly. "Where were you? I didn't see anyone else around."

"I was watching from the edge of the gully."

"And you told no one?"

Kelly hung his head. "No, sir. I was afraid. I wasn't supposed to be there. I didn't know what they'd do to me if anybody found out I'd been hiding in the gully."

"How long had you been there?"

Kelly shrugged his shoulders. "I dunno. A long time, I guess."

Rafe spoke up. "He was living in a cave. I happened to run across it."

Dan closed his eyes and mouthed the word "cave."

Kelly turned back to Rafe. "Guess what? Mandy says that I can come to Dallas and live with her. She knows these people and she talked to them about me and she said she'd be 'sponsible for me."

"That's very generous of Mandy," Rafe said.

"Yes. I told her I could help pay some of her bills if I got a job, but she said I have to go to school. She said there aren't any ranches in Dallas for me to work on."

"Well, maybe Dan will let you work on his ranch during the summers. That might work."

"Where will you be, Rafe?"

"I'll be back at my job overseas."

Kelly's face fell. "Oh."

Mandy spoke for the first time since she'd learned about Dan's injury. Rafe could see she was still upset with him for keeping the news from her. "We need to go and let you get some rest, Dan. Have they said when they're going to let you come home?"

He frowned. "When my temperature's normal, whenever that is," he said, sounding disgusted.

"I'll stay until you can get around all right," Mandy said.

Dan looked at Rafe. "How about you?"

"It's your call. You wrote the letter."

"Right. We'll deal with all of that once I'm out of here."

"I'll see you later, then." He looked at Kelly. "You want to head back to the ranch with me, cowboy? Tom's probably got all kinds of work for you to do."

Kelly pulled on his belt, settling his jeans on his hips. "I'm ready," he said with just a hint of a swagger.

When Rafe reached his side, Kelly confidently took his hand and they walked out together.

Mandy could feel Dan's eyes on her. She turned to him and smiled. "I guess reaction is setting in now that I know you're okay. I was so scared when you disappeared. Then I found Rafe's note when we got home that you were in the hospital. I didn't know what to think." She took his hand in both of hers. "Are you sure you're all right?"

"I will be soon enough." He shifted and with the obvious intent of changing the subject, said, "It's good to see Rafe again, isn't it? It's been a while."

"Yes."

"He's looking good."

"Uh-huh."

"And you're still in love with him," Dan said.

She dropped his hand. "Don't be silly."

"You think I didn't feel the sizzle between the two of you? Remember, I'm the guy lying on the bed between you. It's a wonder I didn't get electrocuted from all the electricity rushing between you."

She rested her palm on his forehead. "Yep. Still feverish…and delusional. Rafe is a friend. You know that."

He sighed and closed his eyes. "He is that. He saved my life."

"I'll always love him for doing that."

"So why don't you convince him to stay here and help you raise that boy?"

She'd been under too much emotional strain for the past

several hours—days—weeks—to be able to control the tears that suddenly filled her eyes. "Can you really see Rafe finding a life here in the States, Dan?"

"Once he's faced his demons, yes I can. He can't keep running from them forever. This trip back to Texas was a start. Can't you see that the man is crying out for a home and a family? Did you see how he was with the boy? As for Kelly, he's got a bad case of hero worship going there. He was even mimicking the way Rafe walks, did you see that?"

The tears spilled over. "I saw it."

"So what are you going to do about it, sis? Are you going to let him walk out of your life like he did twelve years ago without making damned sure he knows how you feel?"

"I love him enough to want to see him happy. He seems to be happy doing what he's doing."

"Yes, because that's the only life he's really known. He's alone. He figures that's the way life is. It's up to you to show him he could have another life."

"I'll try."

"Uh-oh. That's a waste of energy. If you try, you fail, because you're leaving room in there to fail. Don't try. Do it. Give it all you've got. I'm not blind, Mandy. The man loves you so much it's eating him up inside. You've got to convince him that he's husband and father material. Right now he hasn't a clue."

She smiled. "How can he be so blind?"

"Because part of him is still that little kid that got knocked around by a father who convinced him he was worthless. He's needed this time on his own to learn that his father was wrong. It's time for you to help him take the next step."

Eleven

The house was quiet when Mandy arrived back at the ranch. During the time Kelly had been with her she had turned the storage room back into a bedroom for him. It hadn't taken much, since the furniture was still in place. She'd washed the curtains, found fresh linens and had the room ready for him the second night he was there.

She'd returned to her bed, knowing she wouldn't be able to sleep in the bed she'd shared with Rafe when he wasn't there.

Now she checked the rooms out of habit. Everything was as she had left it this morning, except for Dan's room. Rafe had fallen across the bed and was sound asleep. She'd noticed the dark shadows beneath his eyes at the hospital.

He'd definitely earned his rest. She wanted to hear the details of where he'd found Dan and how he'd managed to get him home. However, she'd probably get more information out of him if she let Rafe get some sleep.

In the meantime, she would keep herself busy planning a hearty meal for her guys.

By the time Kelly showed up to eat, the meal was warming in the oven and Rafe hadn't stirred.

"Hi!" Kelly said. "I went with Tom to look for cattle. Boy, was that fun. There's lots of things to do on a ranch, isn't there?"

"Yes, there is. Are you ready to eat?"

He looked down at his dusty clothes. "Maybe I should get cleaned up first."

"That's a good idea. When you've showered and changed, why don't you wake up Rafe so he can eat."

"He's asleep? Already?" He looked at the clock.

"Remember he was up all last night. I have a hunch that cave isn't real comfortable to sleep in."

Kelly grinned. "Not as comfortable as a bed."

"That's what I figured."

She finished setting the table and took the food out of the oven and placed it on the table. She enjoyed preparing meals for hungry appetites. It got so lonely cooking for one. She was looking forward to having Kelly with her.

Her thoughts returned to her conversation with Dan. Don't try, he'd said. Do it. Don't give yourself an out. Convince Rafe he deserved a family.

The question was how.

She heard voices and knew that Rafe was now up. He paused in the doorway and looked at her. "Why didn't you wake me up sooner?" he asked a little sheepishly. "I didn't need to sleep all day."

"I have a hunch your body thought differently. You've been under the strain of looking for Dan for several days. With that worry gone, you were ready to crash." She nodded to the table. "Sit down. Everything's ready."

Mandy watched Rafe and Kelly interact all through dinner. Rafe patiently listened to Kelly's interminable stories about everything he had seen and everything he had done and everything he had thought about doing since the last time he'd seen him, which was only the day before. Mandy wondered what Kelly would do if he had to catch him up on months…or years?

Rafe listened with a keen ear, asking a question now and again, helping the boy to find a word to describe something. Mandy wondered if Kelly had ever had a male figure in his life. What kind of mother had he had? Was she one who got involved with a man, then moved on to another one? Or had her experience with Kelly's father discouraged her from seeking out further male companionship?

She would probably never know. Kelly had talked about his mother a lot once he opened up, but he had never mentioned a man in their lives. She knew that it was going to be a real wrench for Kelly when Rafe left.

At least she'd had years to learn to cope with those feelings, plus an education in a field that offered additional tools. She still wondered how she could let Rafe walk out of her life for the second time without emotionally falling apart.

"Right, Mandy?" Kelly asked, looking at her for confirmation.

"I'm sorry, Kelly. I guess my mind was drifting."

"You told me that maybe when we go to Dallas that I could have a dog like Ranger."

"Well, maybe not exactly like Ranger. He's a big dog, and big dogs don't like to stay in apartments. They need plenty of room to run and play."

"So do little boys," Rafe quietly added.

"Good point. Maybe I'd better be thinking about finding a larger place…a house, maybe, with a yard."

He smiled at her and went back to eating.

By the time dinner was over, Kelly's nose was almost resting on the table.

"Why don't you go on to bed, Kelly?" Rafe said. "Morning comes awfully early these days."

Kelly nodded, his eyelids drooping. He slipped out of his chair and headed for the door. "'Night, Mandy. 'Night, Rafe," he said over his shoulder.

When Mandy began to clear the table, Rafe helped. Between the two of them, the kitchen was gleaming in no time at all.

Mandy followed Rafe into the den where he generally watched the news. She waited for a commercial break and said, "Have you noticed that Kelly very rarely touches anyone?"

Rafe glanced at her and smiled.

"Oh, I noticed."

"I keep wanting to hug him."

"He's got his own space that he guards. He feels that's what keeps him strong. He's not quite ready to lose it. He's feeling his way with all of this. Actually you've worked miracles on the sullen boy I found hiding out in a cave."

"Sullen? Kelly? He could talk the ears off a row of corn."

"You're really good with children, but I guess you already know that. Why else would you have chosen the field you did?"

"Why else, indeed?" She smiled at him. "You're looking a little more rested. I want to hear all about how you did it."

"Did what?"

"Found Dan."

"I hitched a ride down to where he was and brought him back. End of story."

"There's got to be more to it than that. I mean, these are the same people who shot him, from what I can gather. They're dangerous people."

"I suppose."

"Did they give you any trouble?"

"None."

"You just waltzed in and found Dan and waltzed out."

"You got it."

She laughed. "Oh, Rafe, you are too much." They were seated on the sofa. On impulse, she leaned over and kissed him. Impulse or not, it was what she'd been aching to do ever since she saw him asleep in Dan's hospital room.

He pulled her into his lap and leisurely kissed her back. Predictably Mandy was soon fretting because she couldn't touch Rafe through all of his clothing. She worked the buttons loose on his shirt so that she could touch his smooth skin.

"I missed you," she admitted between kisses. "So much."

He looked at her in surprise. "You saw me every day," he said as though reminding her of the obvious.

"But I couldn't touch you. Kelly was always there. I would peek in sometimes and watch you sleep. It was quite a temptation not to crawl into bed with you and wake you up."

"Maybe you should show me what you had in mind," he said, lifting her off his lap and standing. He walked over to the television and turned it off, then held out his hand to her. He raised his brow in silent inquiry.

She didn't consider saying no.

Being with Rafe was like watching a brushfire explode with energy and movement and power. She lost all sense of self when she was with him. She teased and tormented him because he'd taught her how. He'd taught her about her own sensuality and how to use it. Their coming together seemed to ignite both of them, driving them to an explosive finish.

Some time later they lay in the darkness, limbs intertwined. Mandy was content to lie with her ear pressed against Rafe's chest, listening to the steady thud of his heart. She could think of no other place she would rather be.

For the first time in a long while, she was at peace. Her worry for Dan was now eased, she was in the arms of the man she loved with all her heart and she had a young boy to care for and tend.

"Mandy?"

"Mmm?"

"Dan probably won't be coming home for a few days."

"I know."

"I've been thinking about leaving in the morning for a couple of days."

"Oh."

"I've got some things I need to do."

"Okay."

"I want you to know how much being here with you has meant to me."

"I'm glad."

"You're one of the warmest, most generous people I know. You always have been."

"Thank you."

"You deserve so much. A good man. A loving family."

"And what is it you deserve, Rafe?"

"I have what I deserve. I make a good living."

"You don't want more than that? Do you ever get lonesome?"

"Me? Hell, I'm too mean to ever get lonesome."

"They aren't mutually exclusive, you know."

He chuckled. "I see you aren't going to argue with me about the mean part."

"It's part of your character. It makes you who you are. You may not want to hear this, Rafe McClain, but I love every ornery inch of you—good and bad—I know your moods and your attitudes, your hard side and your soft side.

You are tough, that you are. But you are also a very, very gentle man.''

"Sounds like a lot of contradictions to me."

"They all make up the man I love."

"I didn't ask you to love me, Mandy."

"I know you didn't. I couldn't help it. It's like a disease...once I caught it, it's in my blood forever."

"Wow. That makes my heart beat faster. I'm like some incurable disease. You really know how to win a man over with your poetic turn of phrase."

She caught his ear lobe in her teeth and gently pulled. "I never said I was the romantic type," she reminded him.

"No, you never did. But you are, sweetheart, in every bone of that luscious body of yours."

She stroked her hand down his body and nudged him in an intimate spot. "You really think my body is luscious?"

"Mmm." He cupped her breast in his palm, flicking his thumb across the tip. "You turn me on like no woman ever has or ever will. I spend my time around you in a half-aroused state."

"Oh, that explains how you catch fire so quickly."

"I haven't noticed a slow burning fuse around you, either."

The flame they were discussing quickly stirred from its embers, catching them both in its heat. Mandy felt helpless to fight her feelings. She didn't even want to.

Rafe was the man in her heart, the one who had never moved out. She could deny him nothing.

However, he was amazingly predictable. When she awoke the next morning, he was gone.

At least he had warned her that he was leaving. He'd mentioned a couple of days. That was a start. He hadn't just disappeared into the night. She noticed while making breakfast for her young cowpoke that the truck Rafe had been driving was gone.

He'd be back.

Her problem was that she had to do something about getting back to work. She needed her job more than ever now that she had Kelly to care for.

She called her office and explained about Dan's condition. She also contacted the local office and made an appointment to see about having Kelly officially released to her.

The rest of the time she waited for Dan and Rafe to return.

And dreamed about Rafe at night.

Twelve

It took Rafe longer than he expected because he was following a cold trail. A week later, he knew he was finally on the right track. He'd been as far south as Corpus Christi, as far east as Beaumont, as far north as Tyler. The trail finally led him to a little town nestled in the tall pines of East Texas called Eden.

How ironic.

He parked Dan's pickup in front of a tidy-looking duplex. The lawn was neatly trimmed, and there were flowers bordering the sidewalk leading up to the porch. Hanging baskets decorated the entire length of the porch. There was a porch swing at one end near the door with the number he was looking for.

He paused before knocking and looked around. The neighborhood was quiet, with large trees providing shade for the sidewalks and street. It looked like a movie set, not like a place he'd ever lived in before.

Rafe knocked on the door and waited. There was no sound from within. No radio or stereo playing, no television. That, too, seemed strange to him.

The sound of a light step preceded the door opening. A small woman with a liberal amount of gray hair interspersed with dark peered through the screen at him. She smiled politely and said, "Yes?"

He hadn't tried to imagine how he would feel at this point in his search. In fact, he hadn't expected to feel much of anything.

Which showed how little he knew about his emotions.

Rafe stood there, trying to say something. Anything. When his throat finally worked enough for him to swallow, he said, "Hello, Mama."

The woman stared at him in shock. She touched her throat with her fingers. "Rafe?" she whispered. "Is it you?"

"It's me, Mama." He fought the emotion down. "You're looking good."

They stared at each other, the screen door and sixteen years separating them—half his life.

She pushed the door open and with innate dignity nodded and said, "Please come in."

He walked into a room that was familiar in some ways because he recognized some of the family possessions and yet different from what he remembered. The furniture was new to him—well made, comfortable looking and lovingly cared for.

There were framed photographs, large and small, on every surface of the room. Sheer ruffled curtains covered the windows without cutting out the light from outside. Scatter pillows added touches of color, as did the braided oval rug that dominated the central area of the room. He stood in the center of that rug and slowly turned, taking it all in.

"Have you eaten?" she asked and he smiled. His little mama always showed her love with food.

"Yes, Mama, but I could use a cup of coffee if you have it."

She waved him to a large, overstuffed recliner. "Sit. I'll bring you some."

Her dignity never left her. He watched her leave the room, her spine as straight as ever, graceful in her flowered house-dress and her neat little shoes.

He should follow her and offer to help but the truth was, he didn't trust his legs to carry him much farther. After all this time he was back home, but it was like no home he'd ever had.

Within minutes she was back, carrying a small tray with two steaming cups on saucers. She set the tray down beside him and perched on the end of the sofa nearby.

"You have gotten so tall," she said, her gaze avidly going over him. "I don't believe I would have known you."

"I would have known you anywhere, Mama. You are still as beautiful as ever."

Her cheeks reddened and she waved him away. "There is so much to ask, so much to try to understand, so much to explain. I'm not sure..." She stammered to a stop, no doubt thinking of the enormity of trying to bridge the lost years between them. Rafe was overwhelmed by the thought.

"I wondered if you were still alive. You were so young and so—"

He waited and when she didn't finish, he offered his own word. "Angry?"

She nodded. "Where did you go?"

"I ended up back near Austin. I looked up a friend from my elementary school when we lived near Wimberley. His family hired me to work at their ranch. I went back to school and stayed until I graduated."

She beamed. "So you finished your schooling."

"I did that." He looked around at the pictures. He recognized the smiling faces of women he recognized as his sisters. "Tell me about Carmen and Selena. Where are they now?"

"They live in Eden, too. Carmen married six years ago. Her husband comes from here. He has a large extended family that lives in the area. He does quite well. They bought me this duplex a couple of years ago. We were living in Corpus Christi at the time. So Selena and I moved here. She met a cousin of Timothy's—that's Carmen's husband—not long after we moved to town and married him six months ago."

"So you finally left Dad?"

She didn't answer him right away. When she did, it wasn't the answer he'd expected. It was the last thing he'd expected.

"Your father was killed in an automobile accident. He was a passenger. A semitruck crossed into their lane and hit the car your father and his fellow worker were in. They were on their way home from work there in Corpus. There was a lawsuit. The surviving families were given a large settlement before the case went to court."

Rafe tried to feel something at this news, but he felt numb. "When did this happen?"

"Ten years ago in May."

His father had died when Rafe was twenty years old. That was the reality. He'd died while Rafe was overseas, hating him. Rafe had carried that hate with him for all these years, long after the object of it no longer existed.

His hate had kept him from his mother and his two sisters for all this time. "You must have moved to Corpus not long after I left," he said.

She nodded. "The following year." She looked down at her folded hands resting in her lap. "Your dad was never the same after you left. He knew that what he had done was wrong, but you know how he was when he drank.'' She paused, thinking about it. "He went into himself after that, as though nothing much mattered to him.''

"You continued to move around.''

"Yes. He was restless, you see.''

"And probably couldn't hold a job for very long.''

Her black eyes glistened with moisture. "I tried to find you but I didn't know where to look.''

"Did you think to check my school records? I had to have them forwarded in order to enroll. I figured you knew where I was all along, but just didn't care.''

She let out a soft cry. "Oh, Raphael! No, it never occurred to me to check with the school. I wonder why they never notified us?''

"Probably because they thought you moved when I did.''

"Oh. All these years you must have thought we didn't care.''

Rafe absently rubbed his cheek. "I was tired of the way Dad showed how much he cared.''

"He should never have treated you in such a way.''

"Amen to that.''

"I am sorry you are so bitter.''

"I'm sorry you picked that man to be my father.''

"So the anger is still there.''

"Alive and well.''

She got up and walked over to the mantel where more pictures were displayed. "I am sorry for many things that happened in my life. I have had many years to reflect on those decisions I made that I later came to regret.'' She turned and looked at him. "I lost my son, which is a very heavy price to pay for choices made.''

"I lost a family.''

"Yes, but it was your choice to leave. I'm sorry for the way your father treated you. When he was drinking he was a stranger, not the man I married. When we discovered you were gone he seemed to lose interest in much of life. He knew that I was very angry with him. I was also angry with myself. I should have stood up to him when he was so harsh with you.''

Rafe shook his head. ''You'd already learned your lesson. I haven't forgotten how he treated you when I was smaller. I figured it was better for me to be his punching bag than you and the girls.'' He looked away. ''But I finally realized that if I stayed I would kill him.'' He returned his gaze to hers. ''That's when I knew I had to leave. I could only hope he wouldn't turn on you and the girls.''

''No. He never did.''

''That's good to hear.''

''He continued to drink, but not as much. In his own way, I know he grieved the loss of his only son.''

Rafe tried to remember the man who had been his father when he'd been sober. He had trouble remembering anything but his drunken rages. They were stored with crystal clarity in his memory. Now that he worked to recall other images he remembered a man who had played with him, threw balls with him, took him fishing. He remembered a man who took his family with him everywhere he went, a man who bragged about his children and loved to gently tease his wife.

He shook his head. ''It feels strange to consciously recall the past. I'd shoved so much of it to the back of my mind.''

''It is only the past if it's no longer affecting the way you live today.''

''I'm sorry I stayed away so long, Mama.''

''So am I, Rafe.''

He stood, walked over to her and put his arms around her. She clung to him. When he eventually eased his hold and took a step back, she looked up at him, her face wet with tears. ''You're tall, like your father. He would be so proud to see how you have turned out.''

"Will you forgive me for not getting in touch with you before now, Mama?"

"You've already punished yourself far more than you ever deserved, my son. It's time to let go of the bitterness and hate. It is time to accept the love that has been waiting for you all of this time. Welcome home, Raphael."

Two weeks after he'd left Dan recuperating in the hospital Rafe drove into the ranch yard once again. He looked around the place where he'd spent four formative years of his life.

He'd come to realize that perspective is everything. When a person's perception changes, his world shifts. He knew that he would never view anything about his life in exactly the same way again.

He was eager to find Mandy and tell her what he had learned since he'd seen her last. She would understand more than anyone how he felt about what he had recently experienced.

As soon as he parked the truck Rafe saw Tom walk out of the barn. He waved and got out while Tom walked over to greet him. The two men shook hands.

"Good to see you back," Tom said.

Rafe grinned. "It feels good to *be* back. I'm hoping that Dan's home by now."

Tom laughed. "Oh, yeah. The nurses begged the doctor to dismiss him before they tossed him out on his ear. He doesn't make the best patient from what they told me."

Rafe laughed. "Neither did I." He glanced at the house. "I suppose Mandy's looking after him."

Tom scratched his head and said, "Actually she was until three days ago. She and Kelly headed north. She said she needed to take care of everything up there. She's been away for quite a spell."

Rafe felt disappointment wrap around him like a cloak.

"Makes sense. If Dan's recovered, there was no reason for her to hang around."

Tom clapped him on the shoulder. "Dan's been watching for you. He'll be glad to see you made it back in one piece."

Rafe grabbed his bag from the cab of the truck and strode to the house. What had he expected, after all? He'd made her no promises. In fact, he'd made damn sure he hadn't made any promises.

She needed to get on with her life and they both understood that it didn't include him.

He opened the kitchen door and stepped inside. He could hear the television going. He set his bag down and walked into the living room where Dan was stretched out in his recliner, flipping channels with his remote.

"Can't find anything better to do in the middle of the day but watch television?"

Dan's face split into a big grin. "Well, *there* you are, you ornery cuss! It's about time you showed up."

"Were you about ready to report your pickup stolen?"

Dan laughed. "Hell, I'd forgotten you had my truck. Sit down and keep me company."

Rafe stretched out on the sofa. It felt good to kick back and relax. "You're looking good. How's the shoulder?"

"It's healing, but it's sure taking its own sweet time doing it."

"You're lucky you didn't lose your arm. That was quite an infection you'd picked up."

"The doctor said the same thing, so I'm trying to sit here and remember to be grateful." He pointed to his cell phone. "Actually I'm back to work, doing my networking, that sort of thing. I just can't do much traveling yet."

"You ready to explain how you got that wound?"

Dan frowned. "I don't know all the details as yet, but I've given the authorities what I know and they're working on the matter."

"So tell me who the man was who flew us back."

"Carlos Felipe Cantu."

"Means nothing to me."

"From what I can gather, and none of it is hard evidence, Señor Cantu is an intermediary. For a substantial fee he moves products from the seller to the buyer."

"What sort of products?" Rafe asked.

"My take on it is whatever the market is demanding. At the moment the foreign market is looking for the latest computer technology. Someone in this area is helping to supply that need."

"Any idea who?"

"Wish I did. I do have my suspicions."

"James Williams, perhaps?"

Dan stared at him in surprise. "James? My partner? You're kidding, right?"

"He wasn't at all curious about your disappearance. I found that peculiar, given the circumstances." He eyed Dan for a moment, then asked, "What were you doing at the airstrip at that time of night?"

"One of my clients from Dallas had scheduled a meeting for that evening. He intended to fly down at the end of the business day. I told him I'd meet him at the airstrip with the Jeep. He planned to stay over and fly back early the next morning."

"He never showed?"

"No. I found out while I was in the hospital that he'd tried to reach me to tell me he couldn't get away, but didn't get an answer."

"So you were at the airstrip waiting, and…"

"And a plane landed. But instead of the engine cutting off, the plane taxied to a stop and two men got out with the engine still going."

"You spoke to them?"

"Yes. When I told them they had no business on my land,

they laughed. They said I was getting my cut for the use of the place. My memory gets fuzzy after that. I think I took a swing at one of them. I remember seeing the glint of a pistol, hearing the report, feeling a sudden fiery pain in my shoulder. After that, things faded in and out.''

Rafe said, ''Hold on. I'm going to get us some coffee. This thing is getting more and more interesting.''

Dan sat up. ''We might as well adjourn to the kitchen, anyway. I'm tired of hanging around in here.'' He turned off the television and picked up his portable phone.

They were sitting at the kitchen table with steaming cups of coffee in front of them when Rafe asked, ''So what's the next thing you remember?''

''I woke up in some cottage where a woman was bandaging my shoulder. Carlos was behind her, watching. When she left he demanded to know if I was really Dan Crenshaw. Since I'd carried ID with my photo he couldn't deny the evidence. He said I wasn't the man he'd met in Laredo to set up the use of my ranch.''

''Did he describe the man?''

''It was no one I recognized.''

''Not Williams?''

''No. Carlos apologized for my wound. He kept telling me he would find a doctor. When it became obvious that the wound wasn't healing he said he would arrange for me to get back home. I have a hunch he didn't intend for me to leave that place alive.''

''That's what I was afraid of,'' Rafe said. ''I'm not certain why he changed his mind.''

Dan chuckled. ''Then you have no idea how intimidating you appear in that Commando outfit of yours. I thought I'd died and was being greeted by the devil himself.''

Rafe smiled. ''So you said at the time.''

''I bet ol' Carlos was only too glad to get us both out of there. You know, he doesn't have much of a staff there, just a few retainers to run the hacienda. I think he figured he was safe enough from any direct involvement—he was just making the arrangements and setting up payments. The thing is, he knows the big guys, but I'm not sure there's any way for our law enforcement people to get information from him. He knew I couldn't tell them much. I don't even know where we were.''

"Neither do I.''

"Carlos also told me that he would find out who had been impersonating me because whether or not I liked the idea, I was involved in his operations up to my eyeballs.''

"That's what I was afraid of. You say you contacted the authorities?''

"Yes, before I left the hospital. One of them told me this was another piece in the puzzle they've been working on for some time.''

"So you're not being held for anything?''

"Me? I was kidnapped. I haven't done anything wrong.''

"Except own the ranch being used for a drop site for who knows what.''

Dan shrugged. "Well, there is that.''

"So is this the reason you contacted me to come back?''

Dan laughed. "Hell, no. The two aren't connected.'' He paused. "I don't think.''

"Tell me.''

"As a matter of fact, it was about my plant security.'' Dan grimaced. "I don't know what's happening there, but something screwy is going on. I thought I had an excellent security system at the plant, but things keep turning up missing.''

"Like microprocessor chips?'' Rafe asked.

"Did James tell you?''

"No. I happened to read an article in the paper. It sounds like quite a lucrative pastime. When I saw the article, I was wondering if that was what was being moved out through the ranch.''

"Who the hell knows at this point. If so, that points suspicion back at me since I own the plant.'' Dan dropped his head into his hands and rubbed his face. "I've stayed in touch with the local investigators, offering whatever knowledge and suggestions I might have. The sooner this is cleared up, the sooner my name will be cleared.''

"So how did you figure I could help you?''

"Well, after talking to all kinds of security companies I realized I was way over my head. I needed an expert I could trust. So I thought of you.''

"Me!''

"You betcha. You've been taught how to get around the best systems invented. I figure you could come up with something that even the experts couldn't get around.''

"You mean you got me back here to offer me a job?'' Rafe asked incredulously.

"Sounds like a plan to me.''

Rafe scratched his chin. "I think you've been on pain medication too long.''

"Well, at least kick it around a while and see what you think.'' He glanced at the clock. "Mandy cooked up a bunch of casseroles and froze them for me before she left. Let's go find one and heat it up. After dinner you can catch me up on everything you've been doing. Your letters never told me much.''

"*My* letters,'' Rafe said, watching Dan get up and go to the refrigerator. "All you ever did was give me hell in *your* letters.''

Dan opened the freezer and took out a covered dish. "Well, somebody had to keep you in line.''

Rafe thought of his recent visit with his mother and sisters. "That's true. Somebody did.''

* * *

Later that evening Rafe brought up the subject of Mandy. "I'm sorry I missed seeing Mandy. My business in East Texas took me longer than I expected."

"Yeah, things are really changing in her life these days," Dan said, settling back with a beer in his favorite chair. "Makes a person's head whirl."

"She's taking on quite a responsibility with Kelly."

"Hell, she's doing a damn sight more than that, didn't Tom tell you?"

Rafe got a sinking feeling in his stomach. "Tell me what?"

"I guess he finally got up the nerve to let her know how he feels about her. She's thinking about his offer. So she may end up giving up her job and moving back down here. Wouldn't that be something?"

"Uh, yeah."

"Probably not right away. She says she has quite a caseload that she needs to handle before turning in her resignation. But she thinks Kelly would be better off living down here and going to one of the local schools."

"Makes sense."

"You know, I had a lot of time to think, lying up in that hospital, and before that, when I was stuck in the mountains in Mexico. It does give one pause when he thinks he might be checking out."

Rafe nodded. "Been there. Know the feeling."

"Yeah. I got to thinking about something that Mandy and I talked about when she first got into this business of working with kids. As big as this ranch is, there's no reason why we couldn't build a center for kids like Kelly who don't have a decent place to grow up."

Dan continued. "With Mandy's credentials and with the money I've been making in the computer business, we could set us up a first-rate home for kids who don't have one. What do you think?"

"I think it sounds like a fine idea. I know what it meant for me to stay here and feel that I was contributing to something worthwhile."

"The thing is, Rafe, we could certainly use your help here with the kids as well as with the security business. You would understand those kids. Mandy tells me you knew just how to handle Kelly and get him to relax and trust adults again. I have a hunch you could do the same with others. Besides, we could keep you so busy you wouldn't have time to miss all those war games you Commando-types like to play."

Rafe thought about seeing Mandy every day, knowing that she was another man's wife. He shook his head. "I can't, Dan. I've got my own life going elsewhere. You and Tom and Mandy will be able to handle everything just fine without me."

"It will take a hell of a lot of work," Dan said, expanding on his idea. "We'll have to get somebody to draw up the plans, decide on how many kids we think we can handle, that sort of thing. Then there's the actual building of it all. I figure while we're at it, I need to see that the foreman has a larger home. A man with a family needs more space."

"So have they set a date—Mandy and Tom?"

Dan shrugged. "You'd have to check with Mandy. I haven't heard her say."

Rafe nodded. "Actually I was thinking about maybe going on up to Dallas and checking on her and Kelly. I need to get back to work, myself. I still have a contract over there to fill. I could fly out of Dallas just as easy as Austin."

"I'm sure she'd be pleased to see you. And that Kelly—now there's a kid who can talk your leg off, I swear. He's a character."

"Yeah. I've really missed him."

"I'd say the feeling was mutual."

Rafe went into the kitchen to get another beer and worked to convince himself that marrying Tom was the best thing Mandy could do for herself and Kelly.

Thirteen

—

"Mandy, where did Rafe go?" Kelly asked for what seemed to Mandy to be the hundredth time since they'd come to Dallas.

Mandy had been trying to concentrate on making a grocery list when Kelly chose to return to his favorite topic of conversation. She sighed, took hold of her patience and said, "I don't know, sport. He didn't say."

The condo no longer reflected the life of a single woman—neat, polished and subdued. In just a few days Kelly had managed to put his imprint everywhere and to claim it for his own. Mandy was thankful that he seemed to be adjusting so quickly to a more stable home life. She just wished she could reach inside his little head and erase all knowledge of Rafe McClain.

"He just left?" he asked. Now this was a new question he hadn't thought of earlier.

His question forced her to remember her last time with

Rafe. "Not exactly. He said he had some business to take care of and he'd be back in a couple of days."

"A couple means two."

"That's right."

"But he's been gone for weeks and weeks. Do you think he forgot about us?"

She hoped her smile seemed genuine enough for a young boy. "Oh, no. Rafe would never forget his friends. Remember what he told you? He's a forever kind of friend."

Kelly scuffed his toe on the carpet, studying the track it made. "Well, that doesn't seem to be a good way to treat friends. If you're a friend you come to visit."

"Don't forget that Rafe has a job he has to go back to, now that you helped him find Dan. Even heroes have to get back to work and to school."

Kelly grinned. "Yeah, but I like school, so that's okay."

"And Rafe likes his job. See how much alike you are?"

Mandy knew that if she didn't get him off this subject, she was going to end up in a puddle of tears. The truth was that Rafe was acting very much in character and she shouldn't be at all surprised. And she wasn't. Not really. It was just that she had hoped for so much. She'd thought that loving him would be enough to help him drop some of his shields. Plus, she'd thought that Kelly's presence had given him a greater insight into his own childhood. It was true that Kelly's mother hadn't abused him, but the system hadn't been there for him and he'd been traumatized to a certain extent.

Kelly's file was a good lesson for her in her own performance. No matter how hard you tried, there seemed to be some who fell into the cracks and weren't cared for in the way that was needed. She had to remind herself from time to time that it was why she chose her profession—to see that as many children could be helped as possible.

"You want to go to the grocery store with me?"

"Yes! It's fun to go with you. You don't have to count

up the cost of everything we buy like Mom always did. 'Course she did a good job of feeding us, but we didn't get to buy many extras.''

"Oh, and that reminds me. You remember those snapshots you showed me of your mom and of you with your mom? Well, I took them in to make prints and enlargements and we can pick them up today. Then we'll get some frames so you can keep them in your room.''

Kelly nodded. "Yeah, I'm glad. I don't want to forget what my mom looked like.''

"This way you'll always have her picture.''

He studied her for a moment, then carefully walked over to where she sat at the kitchen table and put his arms around her neck. "Thank you, Mandy. I'm glad I got friends like you.''

Dan had insisted that Rafe drive his truck up to Dallas. He said that he or Tom would bring it back on one of their trips to visit Mandy.

After spending another week with Dan, Rafe knew that it was time for him to return to his old life. The problem was, he could scarcely relate to it anymore.

Another perception shift.

Dan had been right. They'd had a great many things to catch up on. They'd sat up several nights into the wee hours swapping stories and sucking on longneck bottles of beer.

It was during one of those nights that Rafe had shared with Dan what he had discovered when he'd gone back to confront his past in East Texas. It had been tough to talk about. He'd had a lot of strong feelings to get through. He'd also had some time to think of all that had happened from his mother's point of view.

He hadn't been fair to her. She hadn't deserved his treatment. Nor had his sisters. He'd denied himself the opportunity to watch them grow up. All of that he'd shared with Dan. They'd talked about everything under the sun.

Except Mandy.

Rafe didn't want to discuss Mandy. Or Tom. Or their future.

Dan acted as though he didn't notice that her name never came into the conversation after that first night.

He knew he was being stupid, looking her up like this, but he remembered that she had asked him not to just leave, but to tell her goodbye first. He better understood why that was necessary. For closure, if nothing else.

He also wanted to see Kelly. Damn, but he'd missed that kid. When he'd seen his nephew and two little nieces, he'd found himself telling them about Kelly, just as if he was his kid, just as if he'd known him forever.

There was no reason why they couldn't keep in touch. He'd get Mandy's address and at least write to Kelly. He didn't want to cause any trouble between Tom and Mandy.

He thought about that first day when he'd been accusing Tom of going after her. He hadn't been all that far off base. She could do a lot worse than Tom. A lot worse.

Rafe followed Dan's directions and found the street where Mandy lived with no difficulty. She lived in a condominium, Dan said, so she would have to put it on the market when she moved.

Since it was after eight o'clock in the evening, she should be home. Maybe he should have called her first but he hadn't wanted to hear her make excuses for not seeing him.

He hadn't gotten around to scheduling his return flight. He had an open return ticket, so he could travel the same way he came back—on standby, if necessary.

After he pulled up in front of her place, Rafe realized that, just as he had in Eden, he was hesitant to get out of the truck and meet the woman inside. He was dealing with his past with a vengeance on this trip.

"Kelly, you need to start getting ready for bed now," Mandy said for the third time.

"Aw, Mandy, it isn't even dark yet. I've got plenty of time."

"Uh-huh. But it takes you an hour to put all those toys back in their box."

"They aren't toys. They're soldiers. Like Rafe."

"Right. Well, they've pretty much taken over the living room and are now laying siege to the kitchen."

He grinned. She grinned back.

"I tell you what," she said, a sudden thought occurring to her. "You can play for another half hour if you'll give me a hug."

He stopped and looked at her with those big blue eyes of his. So expressive. "A hug?" he repeated as though he'd never heard the word.

"That's right. Just like the one I got this morning. I've discovered I'm getting an addiction for the things."

He looked at her with a very sober expression. Then he grinned widely. "It's a deal!" He dashed across the room and threw his arms around her waist. She hugged him back. Then he raced back to his soldiers and was immediately engrossed in his games once again.

Maybe he'd lived out in the wilds too long. She wasn't sure what had gotten him so interested in the idea of soldiering. She knew that Rafe hadn't told him much about what he did, but he had spent time with Dan. She'd have to check with her brother to see what kind of tales he'd been feeding Kelly.

Mandy sank down on the couch, content to watch him play while she was supposed to be going through some of her case files.

She'd forgotten how noisy and hot and humid the city was. The traffic made the Austin congestion seem a dream. How had she managed to live here for so many years?

Now she couldn't wait to get her affairs in order and move back to the ranch. Kelly was already talking about the kind of dog he was going to get as soon as they moved.

She hoped to get him settled in school in Wimberley, but that was going to be cutting things close to get moved so quickly.

Forcing her attention back to the open file in front of her, Mandy began to read and make notes. When the doorbell rang, she jumped. She rarely had callers, especially at this time of day.

"I'll get it," Kelly said, racing toward the door. He never walked anywhere when he could run.

"Oh, no, you won't," she said firmly, rising. "We don't know who it is, so we don't open the door until we find out, remember?"

"Oh, yeah."

She went to the security view and peered out. No. She couldn't believe it.

"Who is it?" Kelly demanded to know in a loud whisper.

She unlatched the door and opened it, standing back so he could see for himself.

"Rafe! You came to see us!" Kelly launched himself at Rafe. Obviously surprised, Rafe caught him up in his arms and gave him a big hug.

Mandy grinned and said, "Come on in. No need to let all the cool air outside."

Rafe stepped inside and she closed the door behind him.

Kelly bombarded him with questions while she tried to calm the butterflies that had suddenly taken up residence in her stomach.

Rafe laughed and swung Kelly around, setting him on the floor. Kelly immediately grabbed his hand and dragged him over to see his strategy with all his soldiers.

Something was different about Rafe, but she couldn't quite put her finger on what it was. He looked more relaxed, more…at peace. That was it. He seemed to have come to terms with something and had accepted it. There was a serenity about him she'd never seen before.

Maybe he was looking forward to going back overseas.

Well, that was fine. She'd come to terms with that. She'd always accepted Rafe for who and what he was. She'd just decided that it was time for her to make a life for herself now and not look over her shoulder at a young girl's dreams.

"It's good to see you, Rafe," she said smiling. "When did you get to Dallas?"

"Just now. Dan loaned me his truck. Said I could leave it here with you and he'd pick it up later."

"That's fine. I have a two-car garage. I'll just have you pull it in. Have you had supper?"

"Not really. I snacked on the way up."

"Let me get you something. We have plenty if you don't mind leftovers."

"I would never complain. Not with your cooking."

Kelly chuckled. "She's making me fat."

Rafe reached down and rubbed Kelly's stomach. "I thought you looked a little heavier."

Kelly followed them into the kitchen until Mandy reminded him that he needed to start putting his men away for the night. With dragging feet, he returned to the living room.

"You've done wonders with him. I couldn't believe the hug I got," Rafe said, sitting down at the small table in the kitchen.

"I see changes in him every day. He really is putting on weight."

"He needed it. He was definitely underweight when I found him."

"He's loosening up with people more. I guess he's feeling more secure."

"Dan told me your big news."

"My news?"

"About using part of the ranch for a special home for kids like Kelly."

"Oh! Well, that's going to take some hard work before

we can turn it into a reality, but it's been a dream of mine for some time. Eventually I hope we can pull it off.''

"And Tom," he added.

"Well, sure, Tom's going to be a big part of it."

"I'm glad. I really like him."

She smiled. "He's one of the good guys, that's for sure."

"I, uh, need to call the airlines and see about getting a reservation. Do you mind if I use your phone?"

"Go ahead. There's one in the den. I hope you aren't planning to leave tonight. You can sleep here and I'll take you to the airport whenever you need to go."

She faced him calmly, determined to show him that she wasn't going to ask more of him than friendship.

"Thanks, Mandy. I'd appreciate that."

"That's what friends are for."

"You've been a good one."

She turned away. Calm was one thing, but when he looked at her like that, she felt like throwing herself around his neck and begging him not to leave. So much for all her resolutions.

She finished making a plate of food for him and placed it in the microwave to warm it. It seemed as though she had spent most of her time since Rafe had showed up at the ranch getting him to eat.

They had come full circle, she and Rafe. She refused to waste an ounce of energy regretting anything that she had shared with him. She had loved and nurtured him as much as she now loved Kelly and intended to continue to nurture him. Maybe that was her calling in life—to make a home for those tough guys who didn't believe they needed anyone.

Only Rafe had convinced her that he was right. He truly needed no one.

While Rafe ate, Mandy went to oversee Kelly's evening ritual of bathtime and making sure his things were put away for the night.

It was at times like this she thought of his mother. Kelly had confided several of the rituals he and his mom had had, asking if they could do them, too. Whoever else Elaine Morton might have been, she'd been a good mother to her son, even if she'd severed all contact with any family she might once have had.

Now Kelly was truly alone in the world...except he had her...and Rafe.

It was a beginning.

When she returned to the living room Mandy found Rafe stretched out in one of her chairs, looking contented. He looked up at her when she walked in. "You are one fine cook, Mandy, in case I've forgotten to mention it." He rubbed his lean belly, at just the spot she loved to kiss.

"Thank you."

She returned to her place on the sofa.

"Looks like you've brought a lot of work home with you."

"Yes. I need to get caught up on what's been happening while I was gone."

"You're going to miss your job, aren't you?"

"A little, perhaps. I'll be doing related work in the Austin area, until we get everything up and running at the ranch."

"Did you ever find out anything more about Kelly while I was gone?"

"Some. We know when he was born and where, from his birth certificate. His mother is listed as Elaine Morton. A father is not listed. Elaine was sixteen when Kelly was born and from what we can tell, she was completely on her own at that time."

"Sounds like she had a rough time."

"She could have been a runaway. The medical records at the hospital don't give much and no one remembers her particular case from that long ago. Kelly has no memory of anyone but his mother. He said she didn't date, but she worked a lot. I can well imagine."

"Poor kid. Not much of a life for a young girl."

"It's obvious she took her responsibility toward Kelly seriously. He had a few photos of her that I had framed for his room. He'd kept what he could of theirs, which is where his birth certificate turned up. She'd kept a baby book on him and carefully recorded each step of his development."

"Kelly's luckier than he knows."

"I'm just thankful that you found him before he got caught stealing. He remembered every item he took and where he got it. As soon as Tom gave him his first paycheck he asked me to go with him to pay the storekeepers for what he'd done. He walked up and apologized to each manager of the store as though they were equals. He explained that he hadn't had any money and he was hungry, but now he had the money and he wanted them to have it."

"I know of very few adults who are that honest, forget children."

Mandy smiled. "I know. I was so proud of him I could scarcely stand there and watch without crying."

Rafe sat forward in his chair and rested his elbows on his knees. "One of the reasons I wanted to come by was to explain where I've been for the past few weeks."

"You don't owe me any explanations, Rafe," she said. "I placed no strings on you. I'm so grateful that you were able to find Dan and rescue him. You have my undying gratitude for that."

"I'm glad I had the chance. However, if I hadn't spent time with you I doubt I would have given a thought to looking up my folks. So I thought you might want to find out what I discovered."

Her eyes widened. "You went back home?"

He shook his head. "It was never home to me...not like the ranch was. The family had moved not long after I left. In fact they moved several times, which was why it took time to follow their trail. I finally found my mother living in East Texas."

"And your dad?"

"He was killed in a wreck ten years ago, which means my mother and sisters were left alone. I could have been there to take care of them if I'd known."

"But you had no way of knowing."

"I guess what I'm having trouble with is that I never made an effort to get in touch with them, despite how I felt toward my father. The news really jolted me."

"I can see that. However, I think it was a wonderful thing that you found them now. Is your mom all right?"

"Oh, she's fine. My sisters are married. The older one already has three children. The younger one just announced that she's pregnant as well. I like their husbands. They're good men. Everyone treated me so well. I—uh—it was tough trying to let go of all this time when I could have—" He stopped talking and she knew just how tough all of this was. But it explained the difference she saw in him.

She left him and went into the kitchen to make some coffee. He seemed more composed by the time she returned. He thanked her for the cup and said, "Tom's a lucky man, Mandy. I know he'll treat you with all the love and consideration you deserve."

She set the tray down on the coffee table and stared at him. "What are you talking about?"

He shrugged. "Maybe Dan wasn't supposed to have told me, but he said that Tom had asked you to marry him."

She sank into the chair opposite where he sat. "I wasn't aware that Dan knew about it."

"Tom probably mentioned it to him."

"I don't understand why. I told him that I thought the world of him and would do most anything for him, except marry him." She looked at Rafe in dismay. "Did you honestly believe that I could agree to marry someone else when you know how I feel about you?"

He looked at her as though in shock. "You're saying you aren't getting married?"

"No. I finally understand myself well enough to know that trying to find a substitute would never work."

He closed his eyes. "Mandy, you devastate me with your fearless honesty."

She glanced at her watch. "Look, it's getting late. I'm sorry I only have the two bedrooms. Under the circumstances, it would be easier—for me at least—if you slept here on the sofa. I don't like lingering goodbyes, myself. If you'll tell me when you have to be at the airport I'll set my alarm and see that you get there in plenty of time." She went to the linen closet in the hall and pulled out bedding. When she returned she found that Rafe hadn't moved.

Mandy set the pillows and sheets on the end of the couch and turned away.

"Mandy?" His voice sounded hoarse.

She turned. "Yes."

"I have to go back to my job."

"I know."

"I signed on for two years. I still have six months to go."

She felt no need to comment and wondered why he felt the need to explain.

"The thing is…well, I've been thinking. A lot. Dan has offered me a position with his company, quite a well paying one as a matter of fact."

Mandy stared at him, her heart suddenly forgetting its rhythm. What was Rafe saying?

He suddenly took a keen interest in studying his hands. He kept glancing up at her for a second or two, then looking back down. "I need to be as honest with you as you've always been with me."

"All right," she managed to get out around the lump that seemed to have lodged permanently in her throat.

He raised his head and looked directly at her, his gaze intense. "I love you, Mandy, more than I ever thought it possible to love anyone. Being with you these past few weeks was like a dream come true for me…and I don't want it to end."

She was dreaming. None of this was happening. Rafe McClain hadn't shown up at her door. She was going to wake up soon and discover this had been a dream, but oh! she hoped she didn't wake up any time soon.

"The thing is, Mandy, I've discovered some things about me that make me really ashamed of the way I've behaved in the past. I grew up hating my dad and yet in many ways I've been turning into him. Not that I will ever drink the way he did, but I seem to have adopted many of his attitudes without realizing it."

"Rafe," she said softly. "Please don't beat up on yourself. You are a wonderful man. I wish you could see the man I know and love."

"Well, my world has been pretty black-and-white. I've never let many people close to me for whatever reason. There's been Dan. And you. I don't want to lose either one of you."

She smiled. "I don't think you could get rid of either one of us if you tried."

He took a deep breath. "I was wondering…I know it sounds crazy, even to me. But I was wondering if there's a chance in hell you'd consider marrying me once I can get my contract taken care of and get back to the States."

Mandy was too stunned to think for a moment. She had never expected to hear the *M* word come out of Rafe McClain's mouth.

She'd be waking up any minute now.

A tremor had started in her body. She wanted to leap off the couch and into his arms. Rafe was asking her to marry him! The fifteen-year-old within her was exuberant. The twenty-seven-year-old was just as excited.

"Oh, Rafe," was all she could think of to say before she launched herself at him.

A slow smile began to spread across his face. It grew and

grew, much like watching the sun peek over the horizon, then spread its light across the world. The brilliance of Rafe's grin could have illuminated an entire universe. In a quick movement, he was up and had her in his arms, kissing the daylights out of her.

She certainly saw no need to struggle. This was exactly where she wanted to be.

He finally raised his head so that they could catch their breath. "May I take your response as being a yes?"

She laughed. "You'd better believe it."

"I don't know the first thing about being a husband," he reminded her.

"Well, I haven't any practice being a wife, but I'm looking forward to learning."

"I'll be back a quick as I can."

"I'll be waiting." She took him by the hand and led him down the hallway to her bedroom, turning off lights as they went. "I'm going to set the alarm but I have a hunch neither one of us is going to get much sleep tonight," she said, once she'd closed the door behind them.

He hugged her to him. "Damn, Mandy, I can't believe my luck. How could you want someone as mean and ornery as me?"

She went up on her toes and gently kissed him. "Because I love you. I never want you to be lonesome again."

Epilogue

Rafe pulled up to the entrance of the C Bar C Ranch, punched the combination into the keypad and waited for the gate to swing open. Once inside the fence, the gate closed behind him as he continued on the road to the cluster of buildings that made up the heart of the ranch.

There had been many changes in the two years since he'd moved back to Texas. It was difficult for him to relate to the closed-off, bitter man he'd been back then when he showed up on the ranch looking for Dan.

Today had been a tough one, but he'd made sure that Dan knew he was there in the courtroom to support him during his testimony. The authorities had eventually arrested James Williams for the theft of various computer components, including microchips from DSC Corporation, and he'd been charged with selling them illegally overseas. That had been nine months ago. The trial was now nearing completion.

Dan had been devastated by the news. Rafe had felt badly

that his friend had to discover how his long-time friend, college roommate and business partner had worked behind his back not only to make money but also to place the suspicion on Dan.

Rafe had spent the remaining six months he'd had to work overseas going over the evidence he'd uncovered and shared with the authorities before he left. In his mind, everything pointed to James Williams. He had the opportunity, greed was a universal motive and he could use Dan to hide behind. He'd passed on his theories to the authorities. Once he returned to the States and began working the security detail around the plant, the investigators suggested he help them set up a trap for whoever was responsible for the disappearance of the computer components.

He hadn't been able to discuss any of it with Dan, not because he didn't trust him but because he knew that Dan trusted Williams and might accidentally give something away.

As Carlos had predicted, the only evidence they had on him was that one of his henchmen had shot Dan. He willingly gave the authorities the man's name but there was nothing anyone could do about Carlos except to file a trespassing report against him.

The Mexican authorities refused to extradite one of their prominent citizens for such a minor offense.

Dan had been shocked and dismayed when he discovered that Rafe had been part of the trap set up to catch James Williams until Rafe sat him down one night and explained that what he had done was to clear Dan's name. Up until Williams was arrested, Dan was their prime suspect, despite his wound. His disappearance actually added to their suspicions.

Rafe left Dan at the office today after they left the courthouse and came back to the ranch. He knew that Dan would have to deal with all of this on his own. He also knew that Dan knew that Rafe was his friend.

Friendship sometimes led to unlikely situations. If someone had told Rafe that in less than three years after he responded to Dan's plea for help that he would be a contented husband and besotted father, he would have laughed in their face.

He turned off the main road onto the new one that led to his recently completed home. He wasn't out of the truck before the back screen door slammed and Kelly came bounding down the steps, racing toward him.

Kelly looked like a typical gangly adolescent with lanky arms and legs. He was going to be tall from the looks of things. He'd taken on a recent spurt of growth that kept them hustling to keep him in clothes that fit.

"Hey, Dad, how's it going?" he asked, sounding a little breathless from the sprint he'd just made. He threw his arms around Rafe in an unselfconscious gesture that never failed to touch Rafe's heart.

"Fine, son," he replied, giving him an equally strong hug. "So is school out for the holidays?"

Kelly grinned. "Yep. And I was wondering if it would be okay if I spend the night with Chris. Mom said it was up to you."

Rafe smiled. "Oh, she did. So what is it that I don't know about?"

Kelly's eyes widened innocently. "I don't know what you mean."

"Oh, yes, you do. Mandy generally gives you permission to do what you want unless it's something she's unsure about—generally having to do with your safety. Now, what's going on?"

"Nothing. Really. Chris is just having a few of the guys over and we're going to watch videos and stuff."

"Uh-huh. And does anyone of your friends happen to drive? And do you intend to be out checking on girls?"

Kelly rolled his eyes. "Boy, you're sure suspicious."

"Which doesn't answer my question."

"Okay, so Larry has his license but we weren't going to go out anywhere."

"I'm glad to hear that. And if you promise me that you won't be leaving Chris's house unless an adult is driving you, then you have my permission to spend the night over there."

From the look on Kelly's face, Rafe realized that this wasn't exactly the permission he'd been looking for. But then his face lightened, and he grinned. "All right, Dad. I promise. I may be the only one sitting there watching the videos at times, but you have my word."

"No doubt they're going to be R-rated videos, right?"

"Dad! Everybody knows those things aren't that bad. C'mon."

Rafe laughed and patted Kelly's shoulder. "Let me know which ones I'd like to see, okay?"

They had reached the house at this point in their conversation and Kelly dashed inside to get ready for his overnight. Rafe paused inside the kitchen to survey the scene.

His mother was placing something delicious-looking into the oven while Mandy was sitting in front of the high chair trying to interest Angie in trying something new. From the yucky green of the stuff Mandy was holding hopefully near Angie's mouth, Rafe thought his daughter showed remarkable intelligence by studying it skeptically.

"How are my girls today?" he asked, taking turns kissing all three of them on the cheek.

Mandy rolled her eyes. "Nothing pleases her. I think she may be starting a new tooth. I swear, she reminds me of you when she gets that stubborn look on her face. Just look at her."

Maria, his mother, chuckled. "Oh, she is definitely her father's daughter."

"Now I'm really feeling picked on," he complained. He turned to his daughter and asked, "Would you like your old man to feed you, sugar?" He took the spoon from Mandy and eased it into Angie's mouth. "You see, ladies, that's all there is to it. You just have to use a little charm to—" He stopped to wipe off the bite of peas that had just been sprayed all over him. "Now, Angie, that wasn't nice," he pointed out while his wife and mother cackled like a couple of hyenas. "Do you want your dad to look bad here?"

Angie gave him a toothless grin and banged the top of her high chair.

He nodded, "Great. Well, maybe we should try something else, huh?"

Mandy said, "Don't bother. She's been in this mood all day. I'll go ahead and nurse her and put her to bed." She wiped his face with a damp rag, then gave him a leisurely kiss. "At least you tried."

"Mama, what have you made for dinner tonight?" he asked, audibly sniffing.

"Just a recipe I found in the paper. Thought I'd try it out."

"I told her she didn't have to be cooking while she's here, but you know your mother," Mandy said. "She can't sit still." She picked up Angie and left the room.

"Once you get the big kitchen finished, I'm hoping you'll have me come help with meals when the children start arriving."

Rafe looked at her in surprise. "Are you serious? You'd consider moving here, Mama?"

Maria nodded vigorously. "There's a nice large suite built off the kitchen area that would be perfect for me. I could still visit the girls and their families but they don't need me and I'm bored sitting around all day. Being over here will keep me young.''

Rafe grabbed her and hugged her tightly. ''Oh, Mama, I'd love to have you here. I had no idea you'd consider such a thing.''

''Well, Mandy's going to need some help…and I want to be here to watch Angie grow up. I missed so much of your life. I don't want to miss any of hers.''

Rafe couldn't speak. He just nodded and walked out of the room. He walked into Angie's room where Mandy sat in a rocking chair, nursing their daughter.

''How did Dan do today?'' Mandy asked him when he sat down in the recliner nearby.

''He was good. Answered questions clearly, handled the cross-examination questions without getting flustered. The defense is still trying to implicate him on everything that happened. I'm glad we were able to gather enough facts to refute that. I guess Dan needed to see that James is determined to bring him down with him in order to realize that man is no friend.''

''Do you think the jury will convict him?''

''I can't imagine anything that would sway them to believe he's innocent. Dan's testimony really ties it up, which is why the defense went to such lengths to discredit him. Instead they made themselves look worse.''

''Dan's working too hard, trying to do both jobs. He's going to have to get some help.''

''I know. He's got employment agencies looking across the United States trying to find the most qualified person to take over James's position.''

They became quiet and watched Angie eat, then fall asleep. Mandy put her to bed and they left the room. Once she closed the door, Mandy turned to Rafe and said, ''Please don't punish yourself for any of this, Rafe. You probably saved Dan from being arrested. He knows that.''

"I hate to see him so torn up."

"Dan's strong. He'll work through it."

She kissed him. Rafe wrapped his arms around her and returned the kiss. Mandy certainly knew how to distract him. His brain went dead whenever she touched him, while every other part of his anatomy came to startling life. He edged her down the hall to their bedroom.

When she finally pulled away from him she was breathless and laughing. "Rafe! Dinner will be ready in a few minutes. Besides, it's not nice to leave your mother alone."

He sighed. "You're right. I guess I thought that being married would cool down my response to you. But it hasn't."

"You don't hear me complaining," she replied with a grin. She took his hand. "Your mother offered to keep Angie for us tonight if we want to go somewhere."

"Mmm. Okay. But the only place I want to take you at the moment is to bed."

"Hold that thought. We'll get there soon enough," she said heading back to the kitchen.

Rafe shook his head, amazed at his own reactions. He was acting like a randy teenager. He had a hunch that Mandy would always provoke that kind of reaction in him.

Who was he to complain?

* * * * *

Don't miss rancher CEO Dan Crenshaw's
emotional love story, TALL, DARK & TEXAN—
a January 2000 Silhouette Desire
MAN OF THE MONTH—
and Annette Broadrick's 50th book!

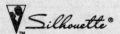

If you enjoyed what you just read,
then we've got an offer you can't resist!

Take 2 bestselling
love stories FREE!
Plus get a FREE surprise gift!

Clip this page and mail it to Silhouette Reader Service™

IN U.S.A.	IN CANADA
3010 Walden Ave.	P.O. Box 609
P.O. Box 1867	Fort Erie, Ontario
Buffalo, N.Y. 14240-1867	L2A 5X3

YES! Please send me 2 free Silhouette Desire® novels and my free surprise gift. Then send me 6 brand-new novels every month, which I will receive months before they're available in stores. In the U.S.A., bill me at the bargain price of $3.12 plus 25¢ delivery per book and applicable sales tax, if any*. In Canada, bill me at the bargain price of $3.49 plus 25¢ delivery per book and applicable taxes**. That's the complete price and a savings of over 10% off the cover prices—what a great deal! I understand that accepting the 2 free books and gift places me under no obligation ever to buy any books. I can always return a shipment and cancel at any time. Even if I never buy another book from Silhouette, the 2 free books and gift are mine to keep forever. So why not take us up on our invitation. You'll be glad you did!

225 SEN CNFA
326 SEN CNFC

Name	(PLEASE PRINT)	
Address	Apt.#	
City	State/Prov.	Zip/Postal Code

 * Terms and prices subject to change without notice. Sales tax applicable in N.Y.
** Canadian residents will be charged applicable provincial taxes and GST.
   All orders subject to approval. Offer limited to one per household.
   ® are registered trademarks of Harlequin Enterprises Limited.

DES99   ©1998 Harlequin Enterprises Limited

Coming this September 1999
from SILHOUETTE BOOKS
and bestselling author

RACHEL LEE

CONARD COUNTY:

Boots & Badges

Alicia Dreyfus—a desperate woman on the run—
is about to discover that she *can* come home
again…to Conard County. Along the way she
meets the man of her dreams—and brings together
three other couples, whose love blossoms beneath
the bold Wyoming sky.

Enjoy four complete, **brand-new** stories in one
extraordinary volume.

Available at your favorite retail outlet.